LUKE PEARSON

HILDA
AND
THE BLACK
HOUND

FLYING EYE BOOKS
LONDON - NEW YORK

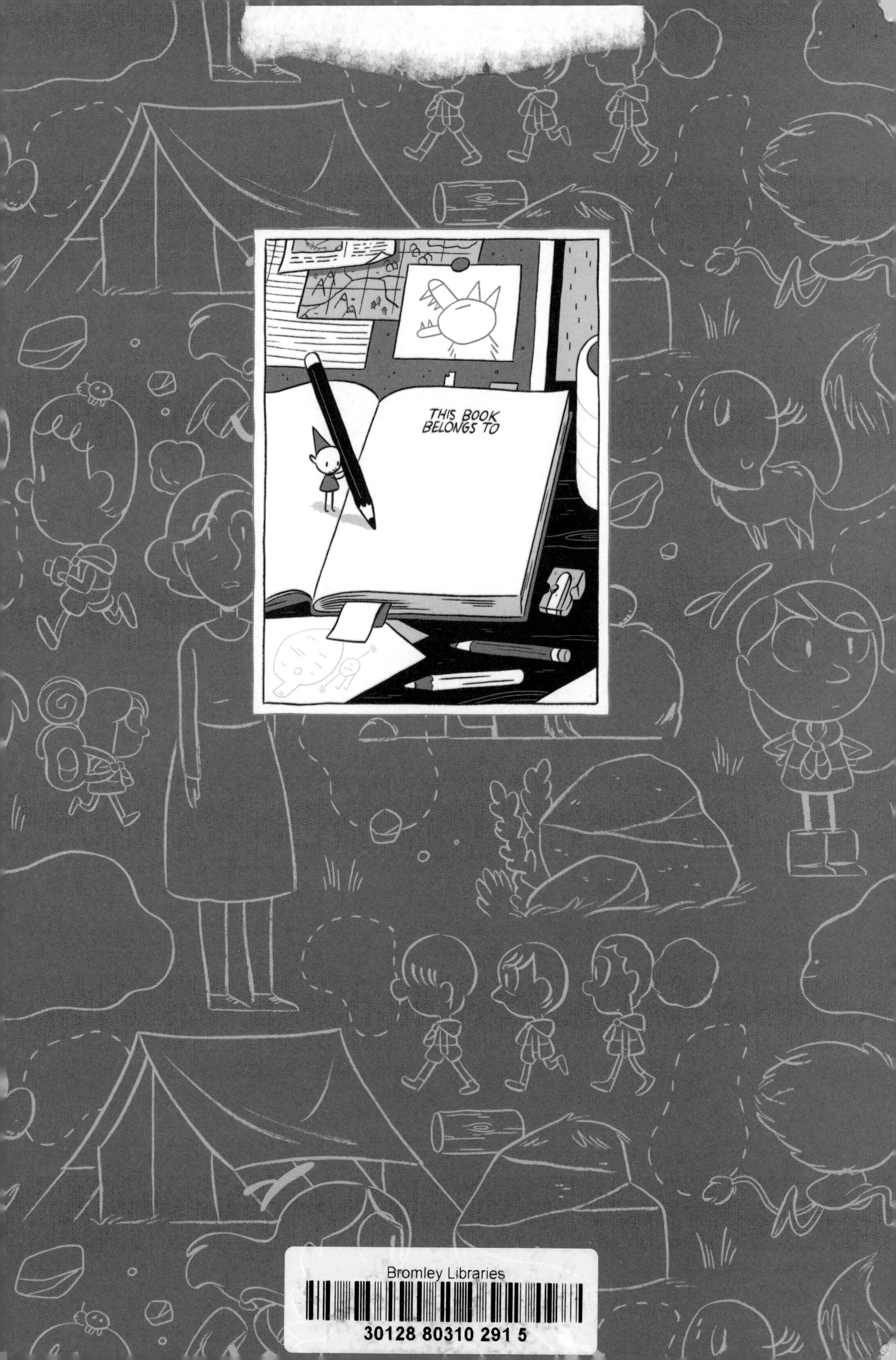
THIS BOOK
BELONGS TO

HILDA AND THE BLACK HOUND © 2014 FLYING EYE BOOKS.

THIS IS A PAPERBACK EDITION PUBLISHED IN 2017.

FIRST PUBLISHED IN 2014 BY FLYING EYE BOOKS, AN IMPRINT OF
NOBROW LTD. 27 WESTGATE STREET, LONDON, E8 3RL

ALL ARTWORK AND CHARACTERS WITHIN ARE © 2014 NOBROW LTD. AND LUKE PEARSON.

LUKE PEARSON HAS ASSERTED HIS RIGHT UNDER THE COPYRIGHT, DESIGNS AND PATENTS ACT,
1988, TO BE IDENTIFIED AS THE AUTHOR AND ILLUSTRATOR OF THIS WORK.

2 4 6 8 10 9 7 5 3 1

PUBLISHED IN THE US BY NOBROW (US) INC.

PRINTED IN POLAND ON FSC® CERTIFIED PAPER

ISBN 978-1-911171-07-2

ORDER FROM WWW.FLYINGEYEBOOKS.COM

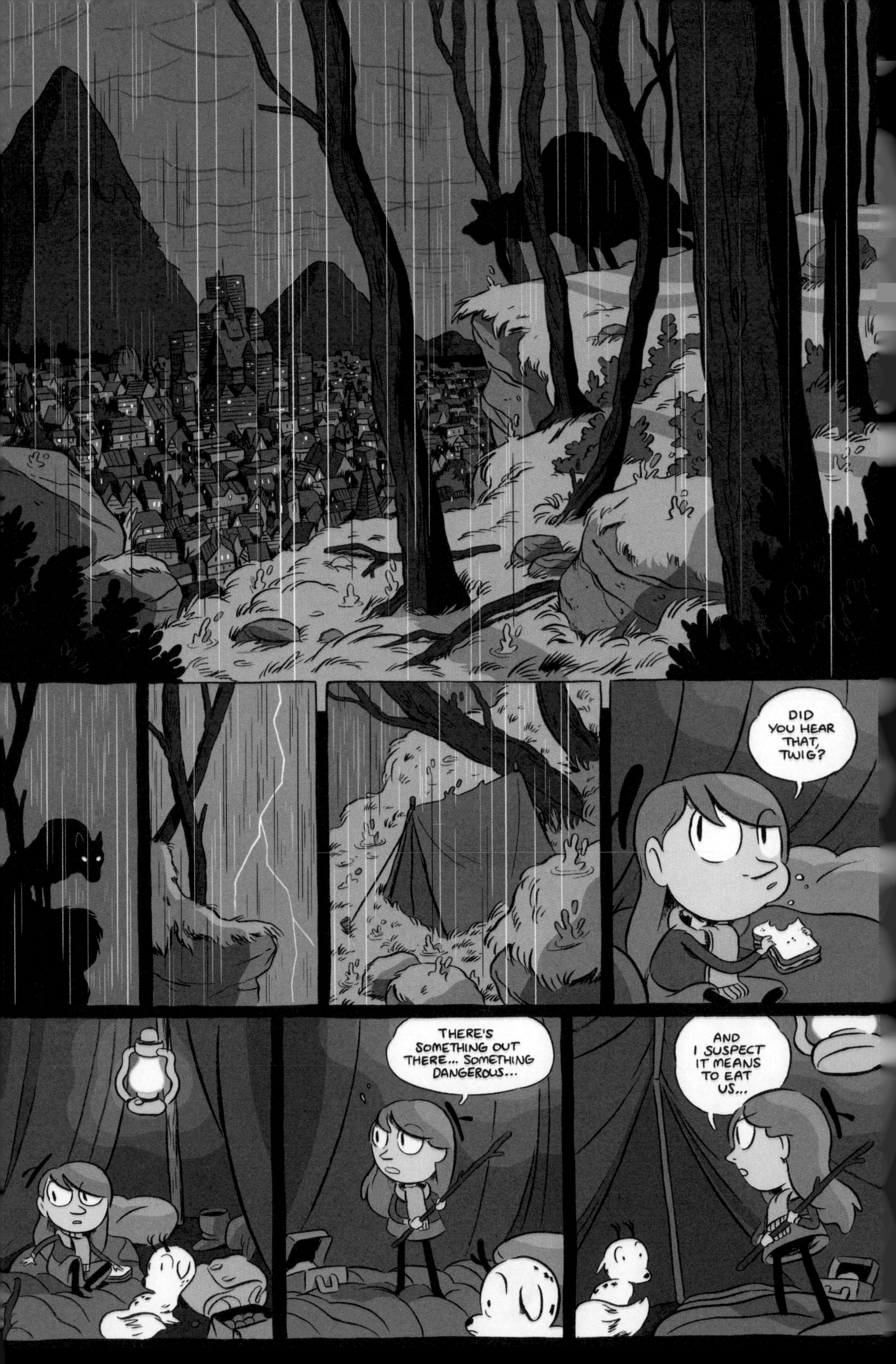
DID YOU HEAR THAT, TWIG?
THERE'S SOMETHING OUT THERE... SOMETHING DANGEROUS...
AND I SUSPECT IT MEANS TO EAT US...

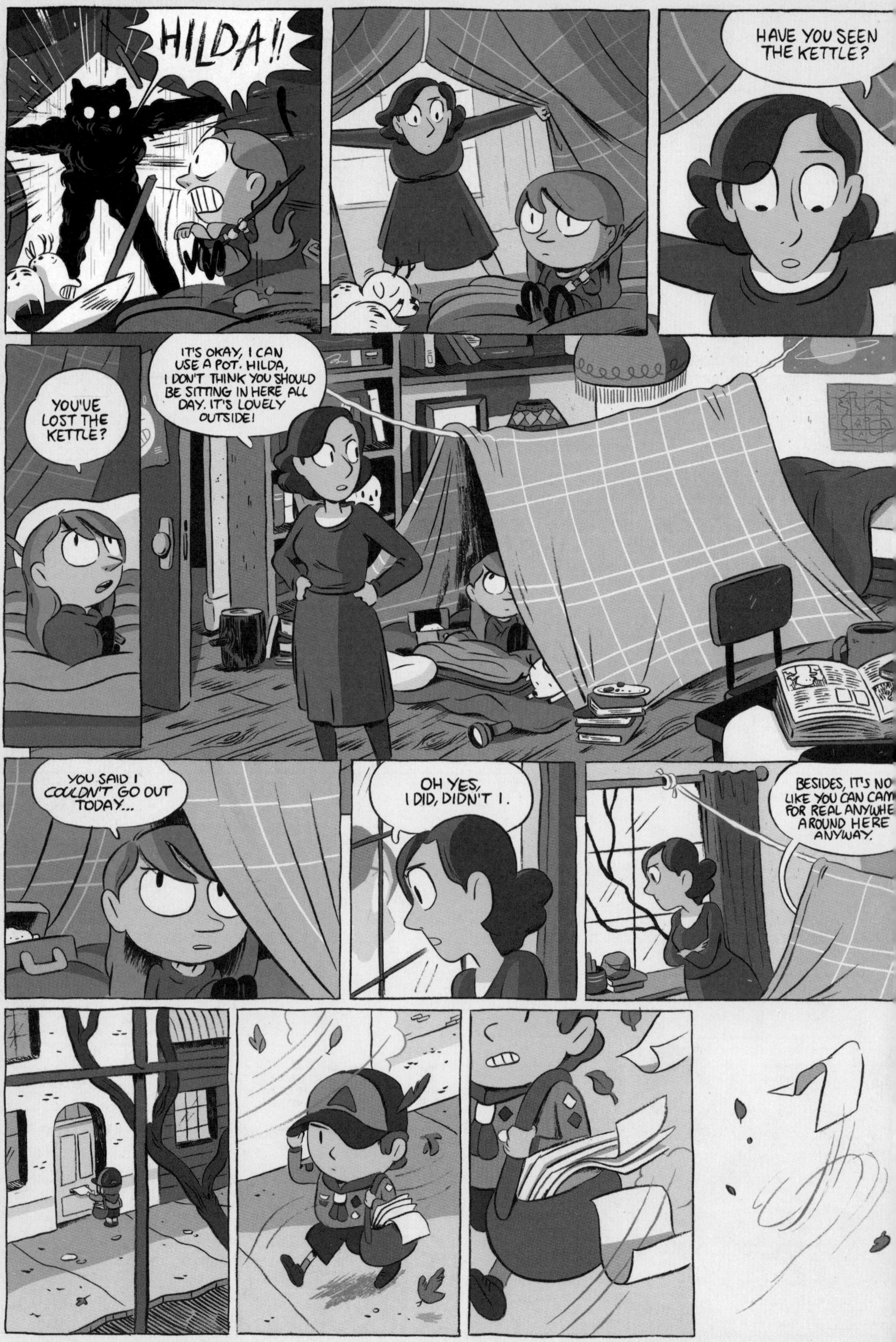
HILDA!!
HAVE YOU SEEN THE KETTLE?
YOU'VE LOST THE KETTLE?
IT'S OKAY, I CAN USE A POT. HILDA, I DON'T THINK YOU SHOULD BE SITTING IN HERE ALL DAY. IT'S LOVELY OUTSIDE!
YOU SAID I COULDN'T GO OUT TODAY...
OH YES, I DID, DIDN'T I.
BESIDES, IT'S NO LIKE YOU CAN CAM FOR REAL ANYWHE AROUND HERE ANYWAY.

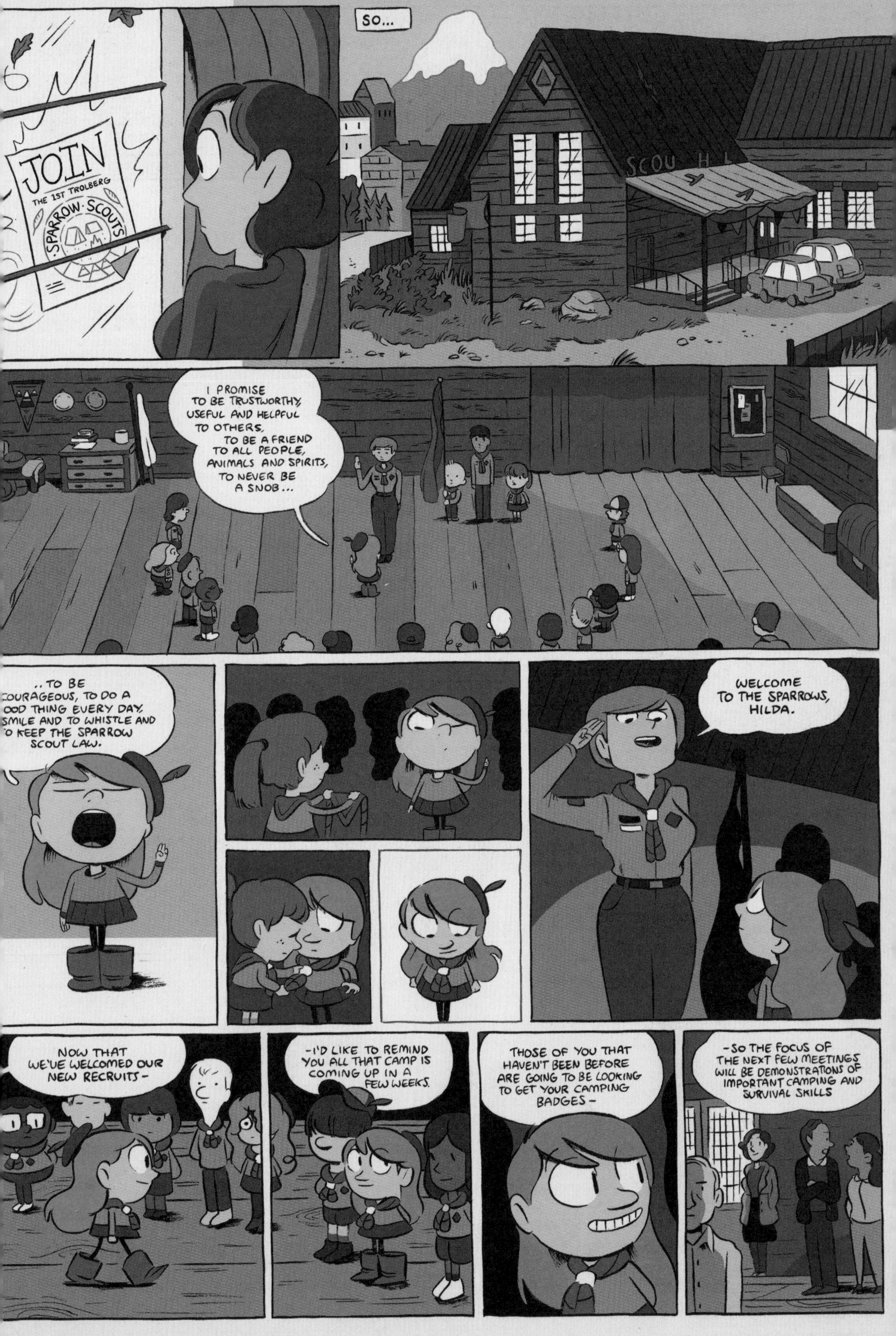
SO...
JOIN
THE 1ST TROLBERG
SPARROW · SCOUTS
SCOU H
I PROMISE TO BE TRUSTWORTHY, USEFUL AND HELPFUL TO OTHERS. TO BE A FRIEND TO ALL PEOPLE, ANIMALS AND SPIRITS, TO NEVER BE A SNOB...
..TO BE COURAGEOUS, TO DO A OOD THING EVERY DAY, SMILE AND TO WHISTLE AND O KEEP THE SPARROW SCOUT LAW.
WELCOME TO THE SPARROWS, HILDA.
NOW THAT WE'VE WELCOMED OUR NEW RECRUITS-
-I'D LIKE TO REMIND YOU ALL THAT CAMP IS COMING UP IN A FEW WEEKS.
THOSE OF YOU THAT HAVEN'T BEEN BEFORE ARE GOING TO BE LOOKING TO GET YOUR CAMPING BADGES-
-SO THE FOCUS OF THE NEXT FEW MEETINGS WILL BE DEMONSTRATIONS OF IMPORTANT CAMPING AND SURVIVAL SKILLS

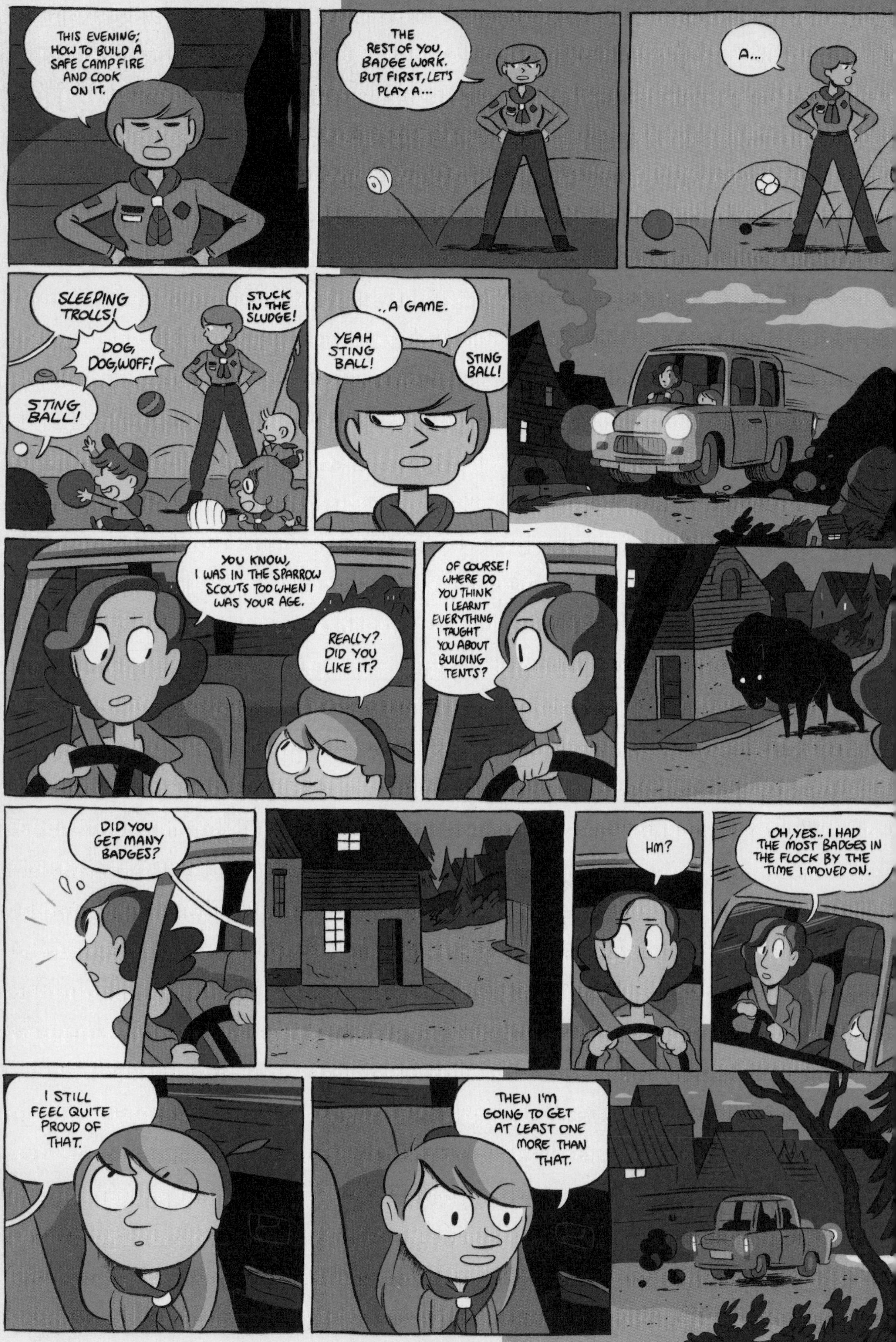
THIS EVENING; HOW TO BUILD A SAFE CAMPFIRE AND COOK ON IT.
THE REST OF YOU, BADGE WORK. BUT FIRST, LET'S PLAY A...
A...
SLEEPING TROLLS!
STUCK IN THE SLUDGE!
DOG, DOG, WOFF!
STING BALL!
..A GAME.
YEAH STING BALL!
STING BALL!
YOU KNOW, I WAS IN THE SPARROW SCOUTS TOO WHEN I WAS YOUR AGE.
REALLY? DID YOU LIKE IT?
OF COURSE! WHERE DO YOU THINK I LEARNT EVERYTHING I TAUGHT YOU ABOUT BUILDING TENTS?
DID YOU GET MANY BADGES?
HM?
OH, YES.. I HAD THE MOST BADGES IN THE FLOCK BY THE TIME I MOVED ON.
I STILL FEEL QUITE PROUD OF THAT.
THEN I'M GOING TO GET AT LEAST ONE MORE THAN THAT.

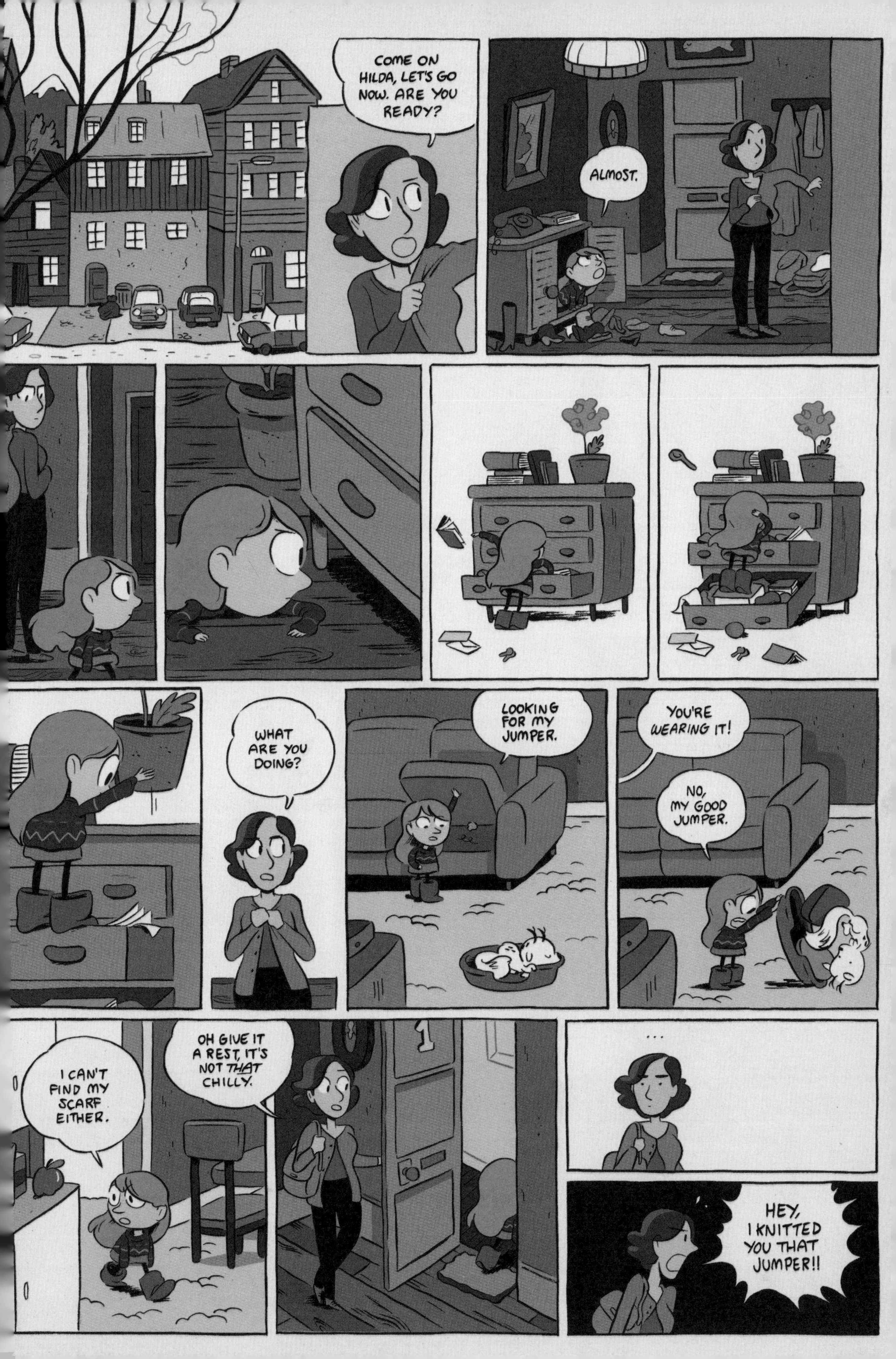
COME ON HILDA, LET'S GO NOW. ARE YOU READY?
ALMOST.
WHAT ARE YOU DOING?
LOOKING FOR MY JUMPER.
YOU'RE WEARING IT!
NO, MY GOOD JUMPER.
I CAN'T FIND MY SCARF EITHER.
OH GIVE IT A REST, IT'S NOT THAT CHILLY.
...
HEY, I KNITTED YOU THAT JUMPER!!

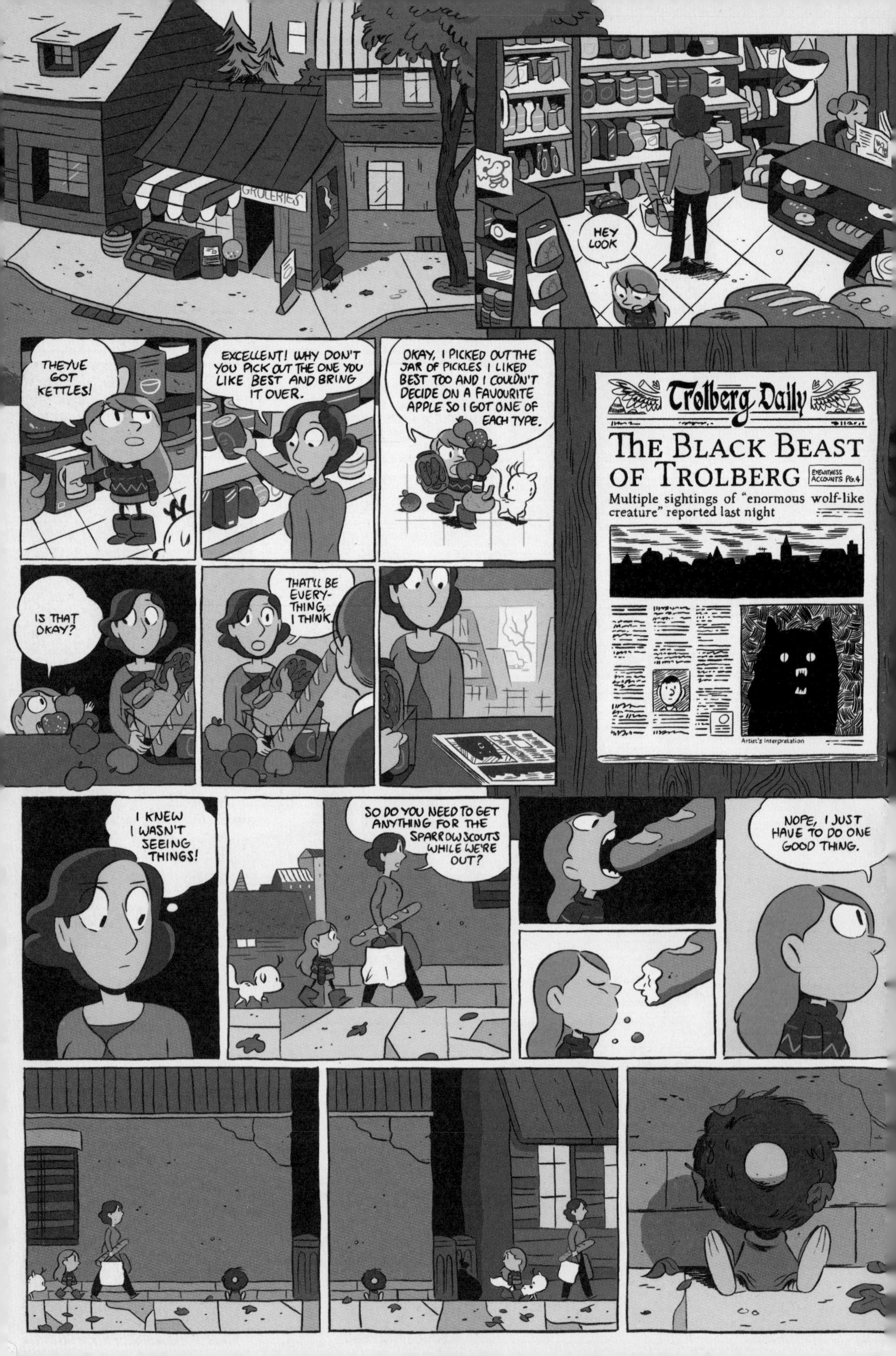
GROCERIES
HEY LOOK
THEY'VE GOT KETTLES!
EXCELLENT! WHY DON'T YOU PICK OUT THE ONE YOU LIKE BEST AND BRING IT OVER.
OKAY, I PICKED OUT THE JAR OF PICKLES I LIKED BEST TOO AND I COULDN'T DECIDE ON A FAVOURITE APPLE SO I GOT ONE OF EACH TYPE.
Trolberg Daily
THE BLACK BEAST OF TROLBERG
EYEWITNESS ACCOUNTS PG.4
Multiple sightings of "enormous wolf-like creature" reported last night
Artist's interpretation
IS THAT OKAY?
THAT'LL BE EVERYTHING, I THINK.
I KNEW I WASN'T SEEING THINGS!
SO DO YOU NEED TO GET ANYTHING FOR THE SPARROW SCOUTS WHILE WE'RE OUT?
NOPE, I JUST HAVE TO DO ONE GOOD THING.

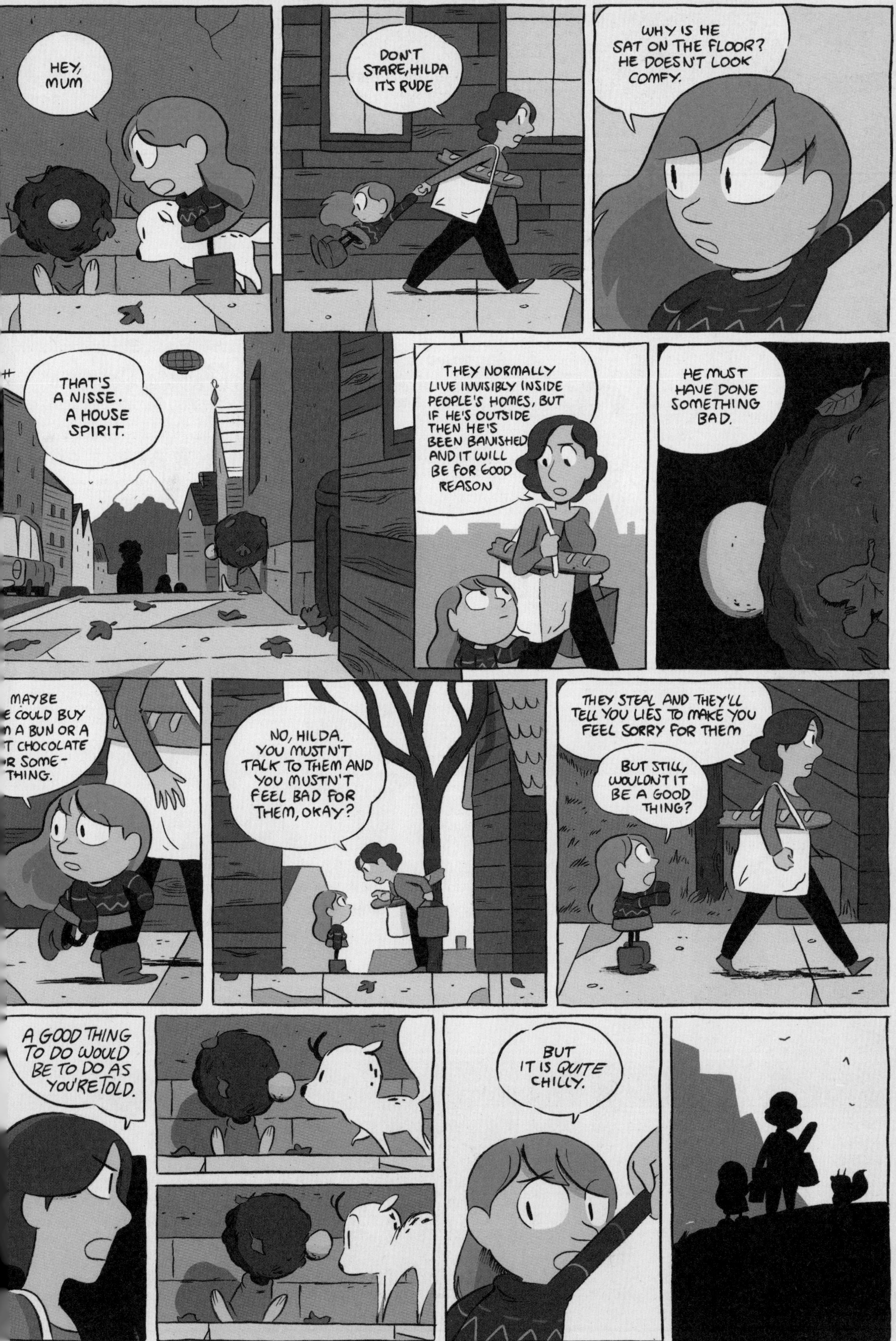

HEY, MUM
DON'T STARE, HILDA IT'S RUDE
WHY IS HE SAT ON THE FLOOR? HE DOESN'T LOOK COMFY.
THAT'S A NISSE. A HOUSE SPIRIT.
THEY NORMALLY LIVE INVISIBLY INSIDE PEOPLE'S HOMES, BUT IF HE'S OUTSIDE THEN HE'S BEEN BANISHED AND IT WILL BE FOR GOOD REASON
HE MUST HAVE DONE SOMETHING BAD.
MAYBE
E COULD BUY
N A BUN OR A
T CHOCOLATE
R SOME-
THING.
NO, HILDA. YOU MUSTN'T TALK TO THEM AND YOU MUSTN'T FEEL BAD FOR THEM, OKAY?
THEY STEAL AND THEY'LL TELL YOU LIES TO MAKE YOU FEEL SORRY FOR THEM
BUT STILL, WOULDN'T IT BE A GOOD THING?
A GOOD THING TO DO WOULD BE TO DO AS YOU'RE TOLD.
BUT IT IS *QUITE* CHILLY.

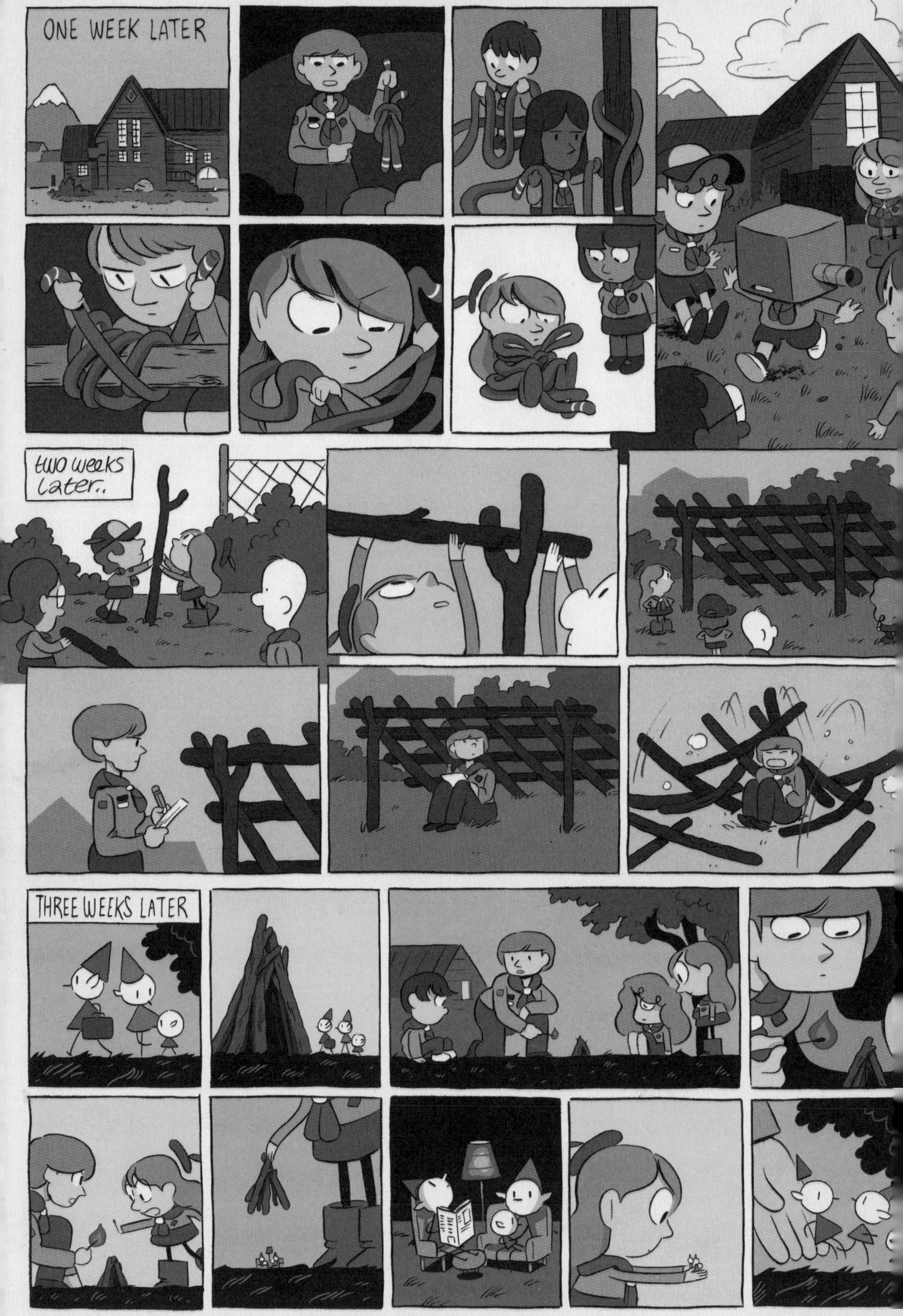
ONE WEEK LATER
two weeks later..
THREE WEEKS LATER

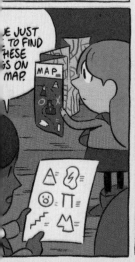

UR WEEKS LATER
E JUST
TO FIND
THESE
GS ON
MAP.
MAP
THAT SHOULDN'T BE SO HARD. THE MAP'S NOT THAT BIG.
E WEEKS LATER
OK THOSE OF YOU WHO AREN'T PRETENDING TO BE HURT-
URRR..
I WANT YOU TO PUT YOUR PARTNER IN THE RECOVERY POSITION
URRRR THE PAIN..
-LIKE I JUST SHOWED YOU
OUCH... OUCH! OWWW
AAARRGHH
IS IT OKAY IF I SWAP PARTNERS? HILDA'S HAVING TOO MUCH FUN
I CAN'T BE SAVED
X WEEKS LATER

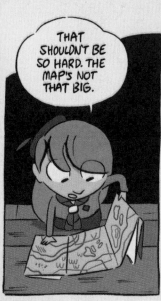

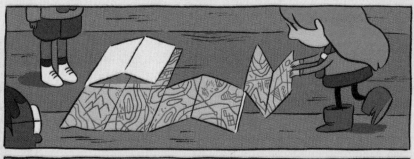

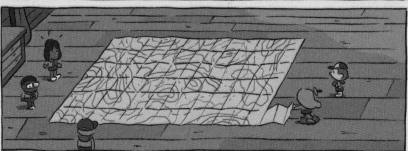

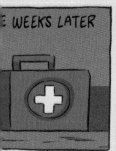

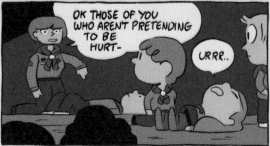

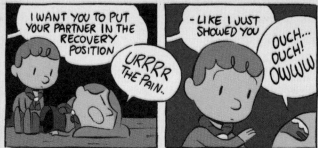

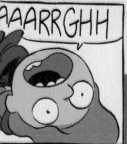

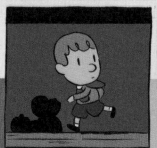

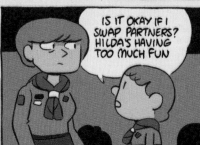

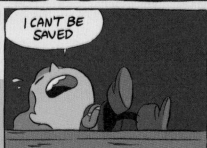

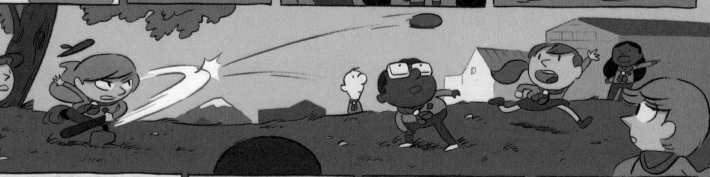

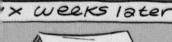

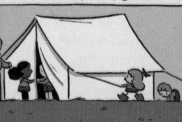

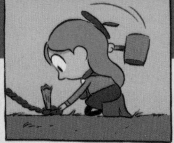

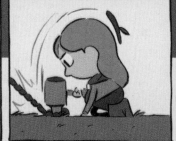

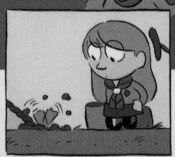

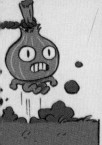

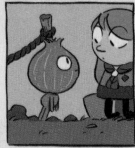

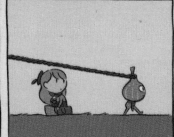

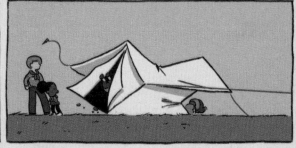

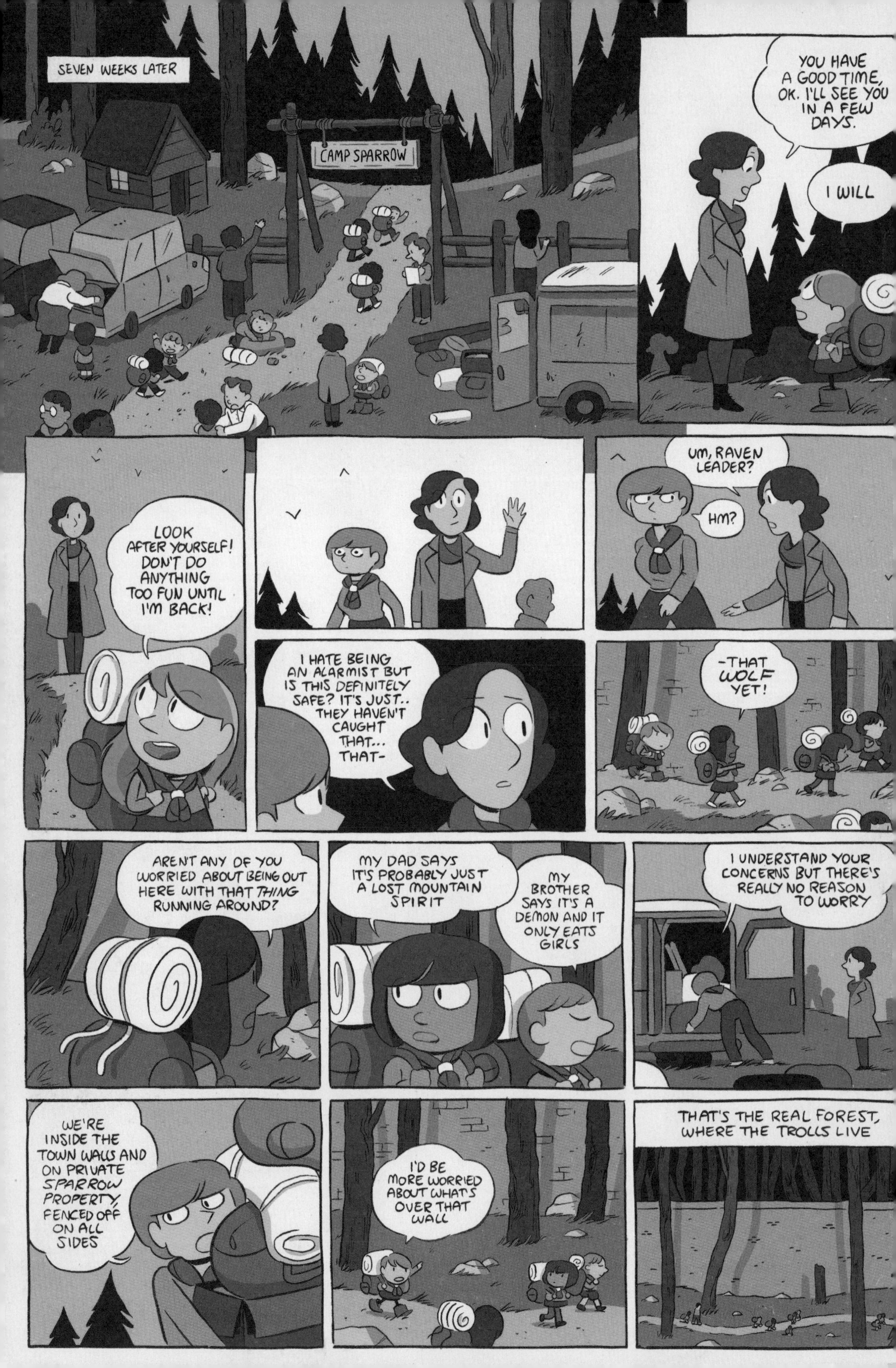
SEVEN WEEKS LATER
CAMP SPARROW
YOU HAVE A GOOD TIME, OK. I'LL SEE YOU IN A FEW DAYS.
I WILL
LOOK AFTER YOURSELF! DON'T DO ANYTHING TOO FUN UNTIL I'M BACK!
UM, RAVEN LEADER?
HM?
I HATE BEING AN ALARMIST BUT IS THIS DEFINITELY SAFE? IT'S JUST.. THEY HAVEN'T CAUGHT THAT... THAT-
-THAT WOLF YET!
AREN'T ANY OF YOU WORRIED ABOUT BEING OUT HERE WITH THAT THING RUNNING AROUND?
MY DAD SAYS IT'S PROBABLY JUST A LOST MOUNTAIN SPIRIT
MY BROTHER SAYS IT'S A DEMON AND IT ONLY EATS GIRLS
I UNDERSTAND YOUR CONCERNS BUT THERE'S REALLY NO REASON TO WORRY
WE'RE INSIDE THE TOWN WALLS AND ON PRIVATE SPARROW PROPERTY, FENCED OFF ON ALL SIDES
I'D BE MORE WORRIED ABOUT WHAT'S OVER THAT WALL
THAT'S THE REAL FOREST, WHERE THE TROLLS LIVE

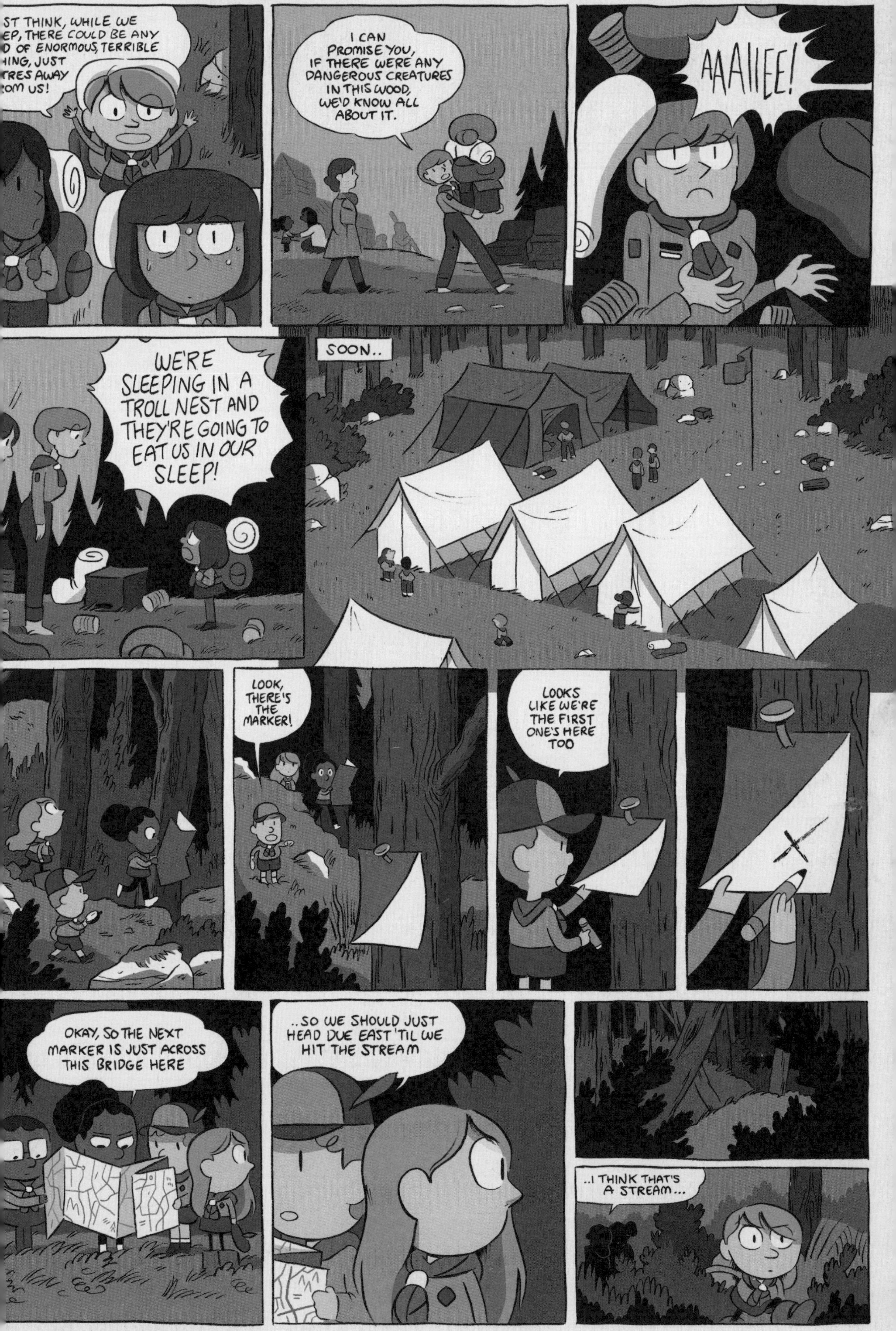
ST THINK, WHILE WE EP, THERE COULD BE ANY D OF ENORMOUS, TERRIBLE HING, JUST TRES AWAY ROM US!
I CAN PROMISE YOU, IF THERE WERE ANY DANGEROUS CREATURES IN THIS WOOD, WE'D KNOW ALL ABOUT IT.
AAAIIEE!
WE'RE SLEEPING IN A TROLL NEST AND THEY'RE GOING TO EAT US IN OUR SLEEP!
SOON..
LOOK, THERE'S THE MARKER!
LOOKS LIKE WE'RE THE FIRST ONE'S HERE TOO
OKAY, SO THE NEXT MARKER IS JUST ACROSS THIS BRIDGE HERE
..SO WE SHOULD JUST HEAD DUE EAST 'TIL WE HIT THE STREAM
..I THINK THAT'S A STREAM...

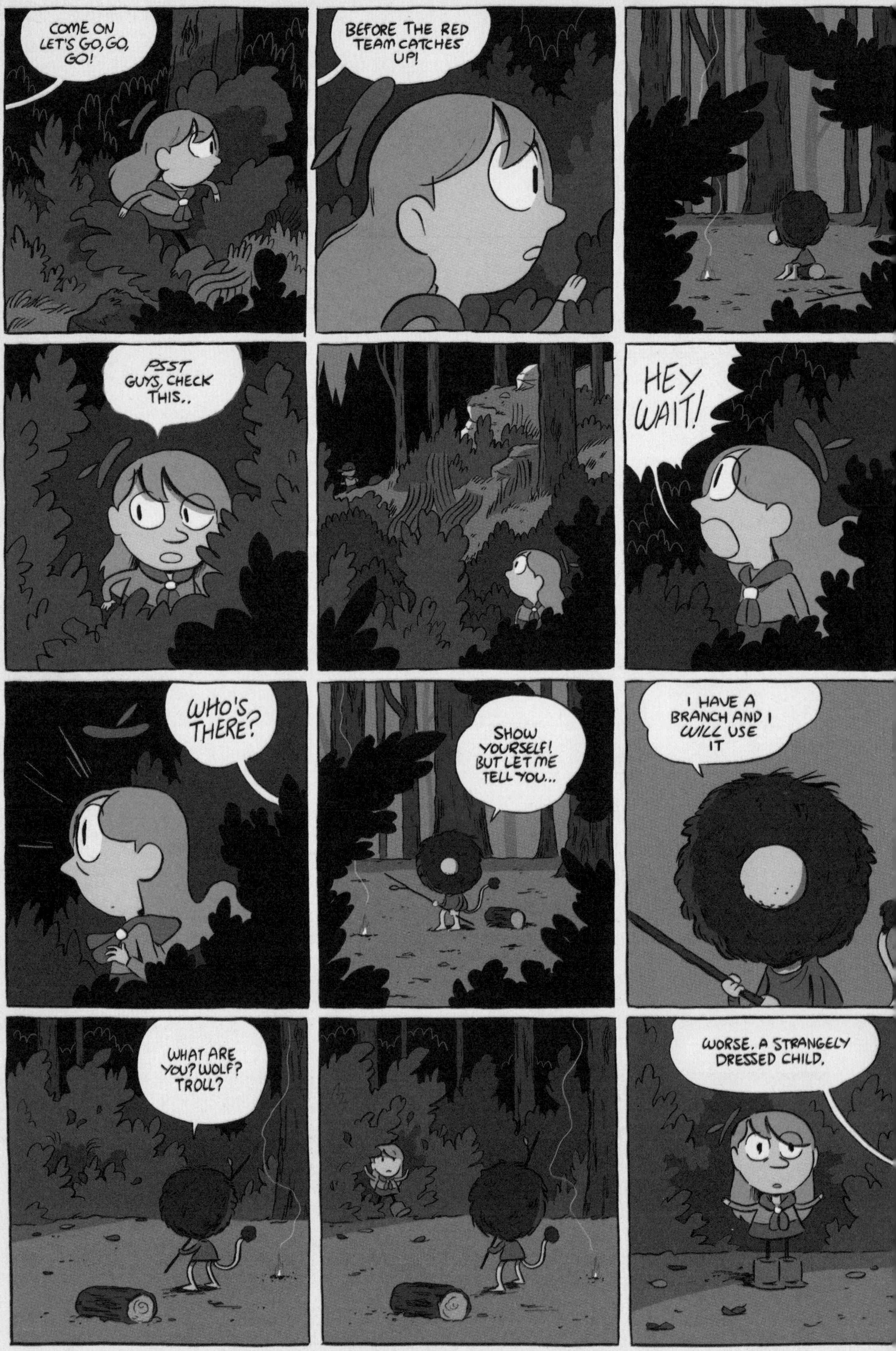
COME ON LET'S GO, GO, GO!
BEFORE THE RED TEAM CATCHES UP!
PSST GUYS, CHECK THIS..
HEY WAIT!
WHO'S THERE?
SHOW YOURSELF! BUT LET ME TELL YOU...
I HAVE A BRANCH AND I WILL USE IT
WHAT ARE YOU? WOLF? TROLL?
WORSE. A STRANGELY DRESSED CHILD.

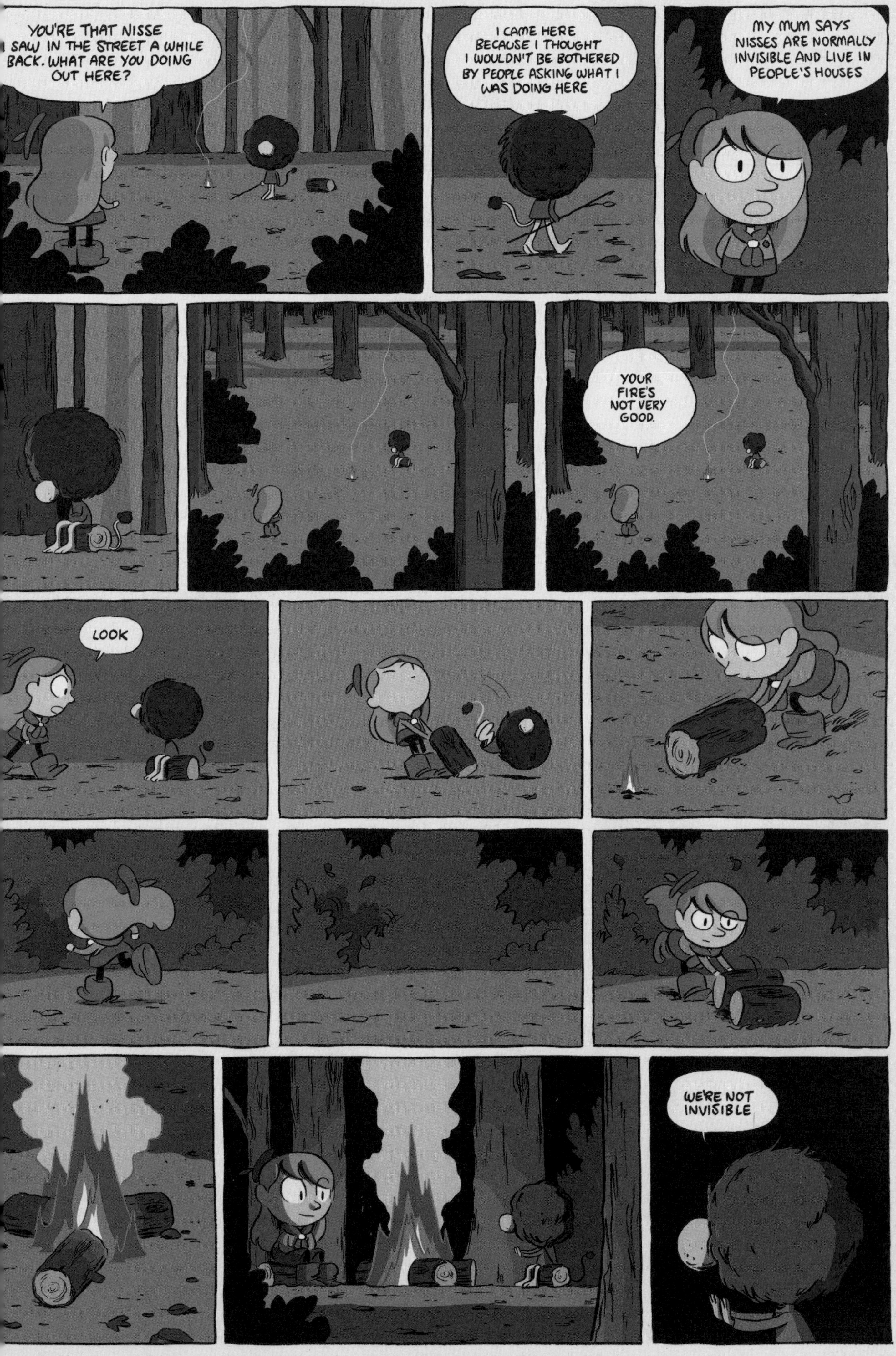
YOU'RE THAT NISSE I SAW IN THE STREET A WHILE BACK. WHAT ARE YOU DOING OUT HERE?
I CAME HERE BECAUSE I THOUGHT I WOULDN'T BE BOTHERED BY PEOPLE ASKING WHAT I WAS DOING HERE
MY MUM SAYS NISSES ARE NORMALLY INVISIBLE AND LIVE IN PEOPLE'S HOUSES
YOUR FIRE'S NOT VERY GOOD.
LOOK
WE'RE NOT INVISIBLE

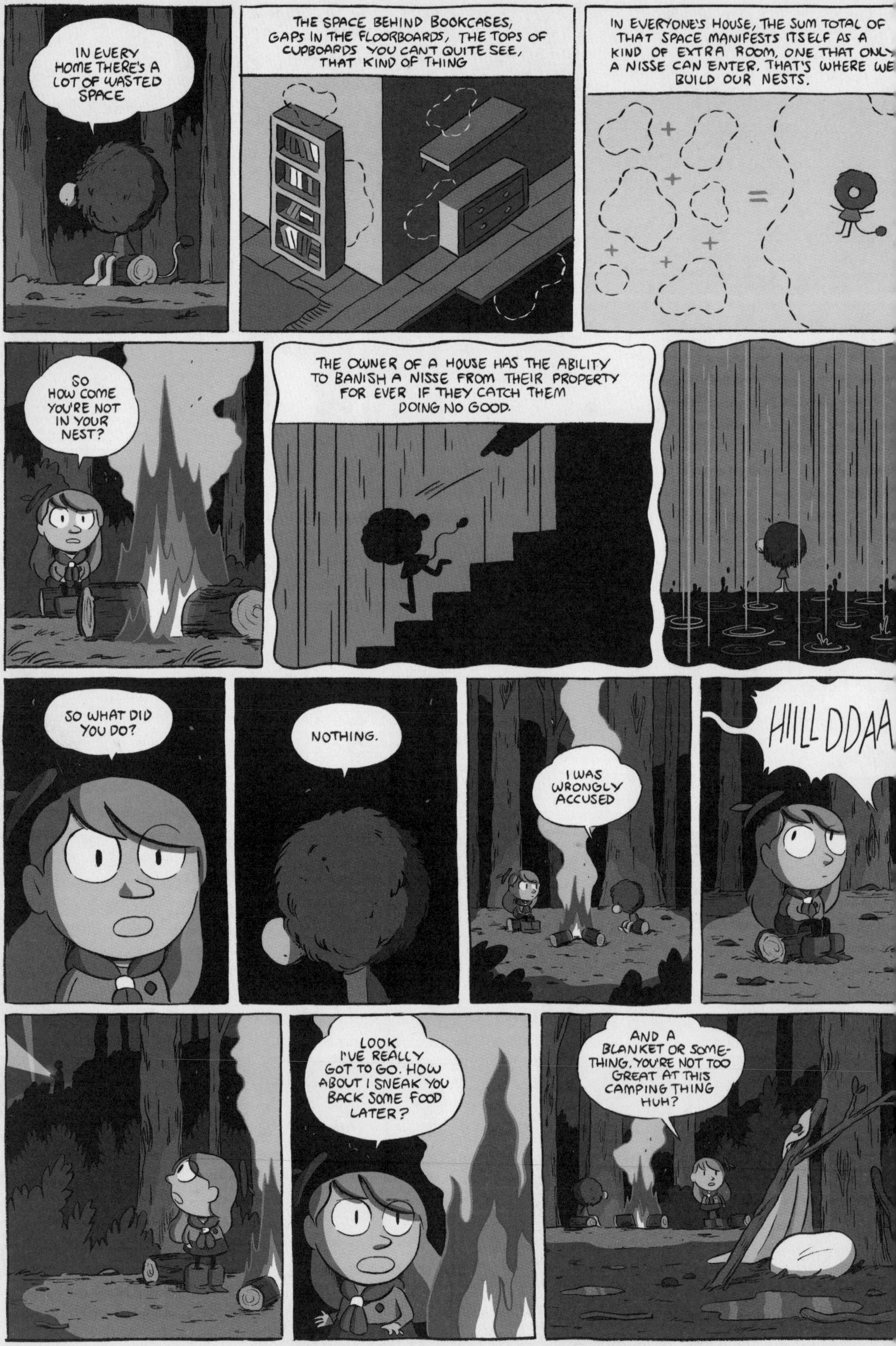
IN EVERY HOME THERE'S A LOT OF WASTED SPACE
THE SPACE BEHIND BOOKCASES, GAPS IN THE FLOORBOARDS, THE TOPS OF CUPBOARDS YOU CAN'T QUITE SEE, THAT KIND OF THING
IN EVERYONE'S HOUSE, THE SUM TOTAL OF THAT SPACE MANIFESTS ITSELF AS A KIND OF EXTRA ROOM, ONE THAT ONLY A NISSE CAN ENTER. THAT'S WHERE WE BUILD OUR NESTS.
SO HOW COME YOU'RE NOT IN YOUR NEST?
THE OWNER OF A HOUSE HAS THE ABILITY TO BANISH A NISSE FROM THEIR PROPERTY FOR EVER IF THEY CATCH THEM DOING NO GOOD.
SO WHAT DID YOU DO?
NOTHING.
I WAS WRONGLY ACCUSED
HIILLDDAA
LOOK I'VE REALLY GOT TO GO. HOW ABOUT I SNEAK YOU BACK SOME FOOD LATER?
AND A BLANKET OR SOMETHING. YOU'RE NOT TOO GREAT AT THIS CAMPING THING HUH?

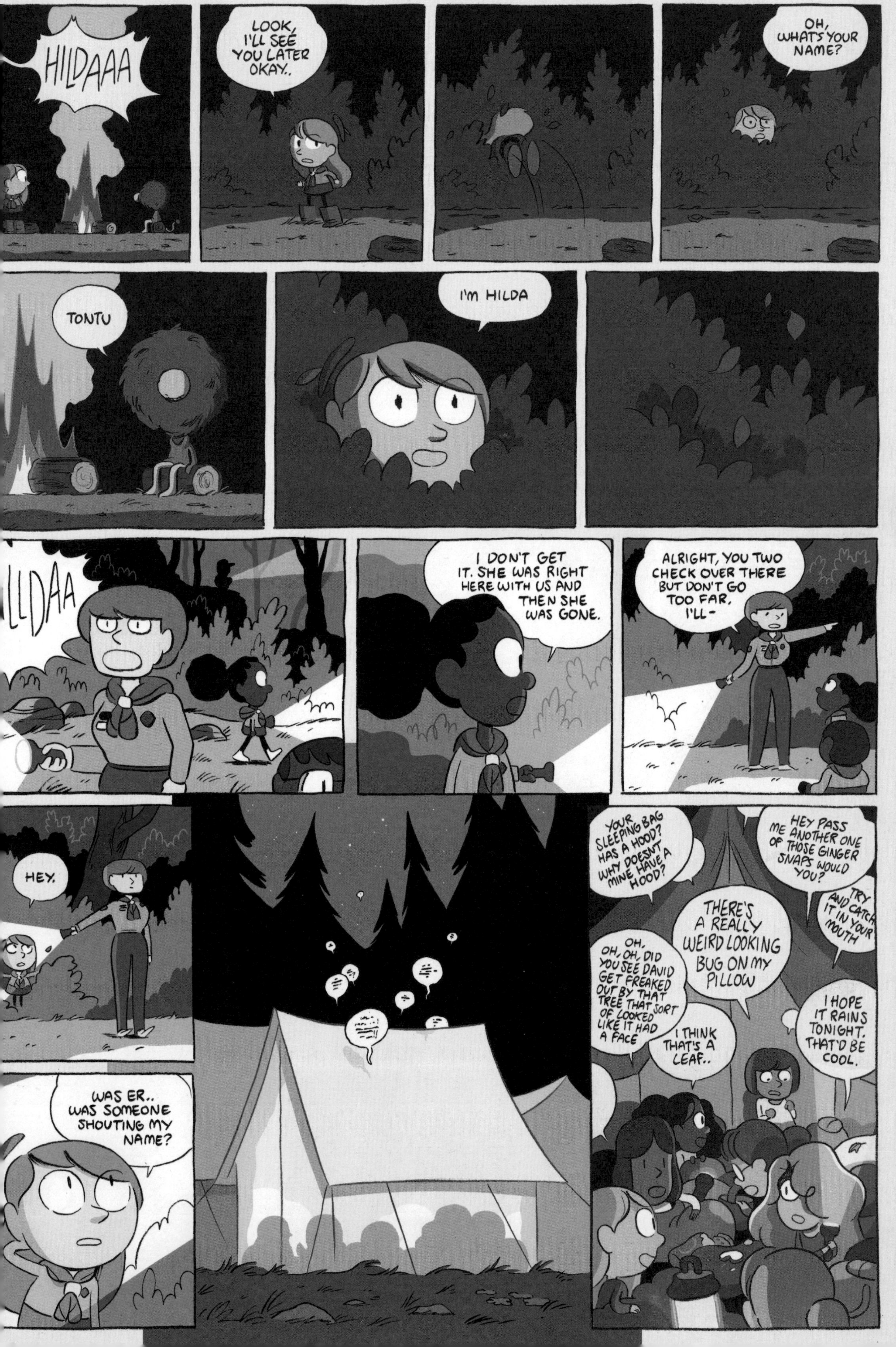
HILDAAA
LOOK, I'LL SEE YOU LATER OKAY..
OH, WHAT'S YOUR NAME?
TONTU
I'M HILDA
LLDAA
I DON'T GET IT. SHE WAS RIGHT HERE WITH US AND THEN SHE WAS GONE.
ALRIGHT, YOU TWO CHECK OVER THERE BUT DON'T GO TOO FAR, I'LL-
HEY.
WAS ER.. WAS SOMEONE SHOUTING MY NAME?
YOUR SLEEPING BAG HAS A HOOD? WHY DOESN'T MINE HAVE A HOOD?
HEY PASS ME ANOTHER ONE OF THOSE GINGER SNAPS WOULD YOU?
TRY AND CATCH IT IN YOUR MOUTH
THERE'S A REALLY WEIRD LOOKING BUG ON MY PILLOW
OH, OH, OH, DID YOU SEE DAVID GET FREAKED OUT BY THAT TREE THAT SORT OF LOOKED LIKE IT HAD A FACE
I THINK THAT'S A LEAF..
I HOPE IT RAINS TONIGHT. THAT'D BE COOL.

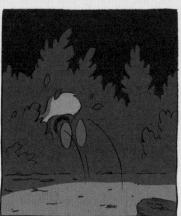

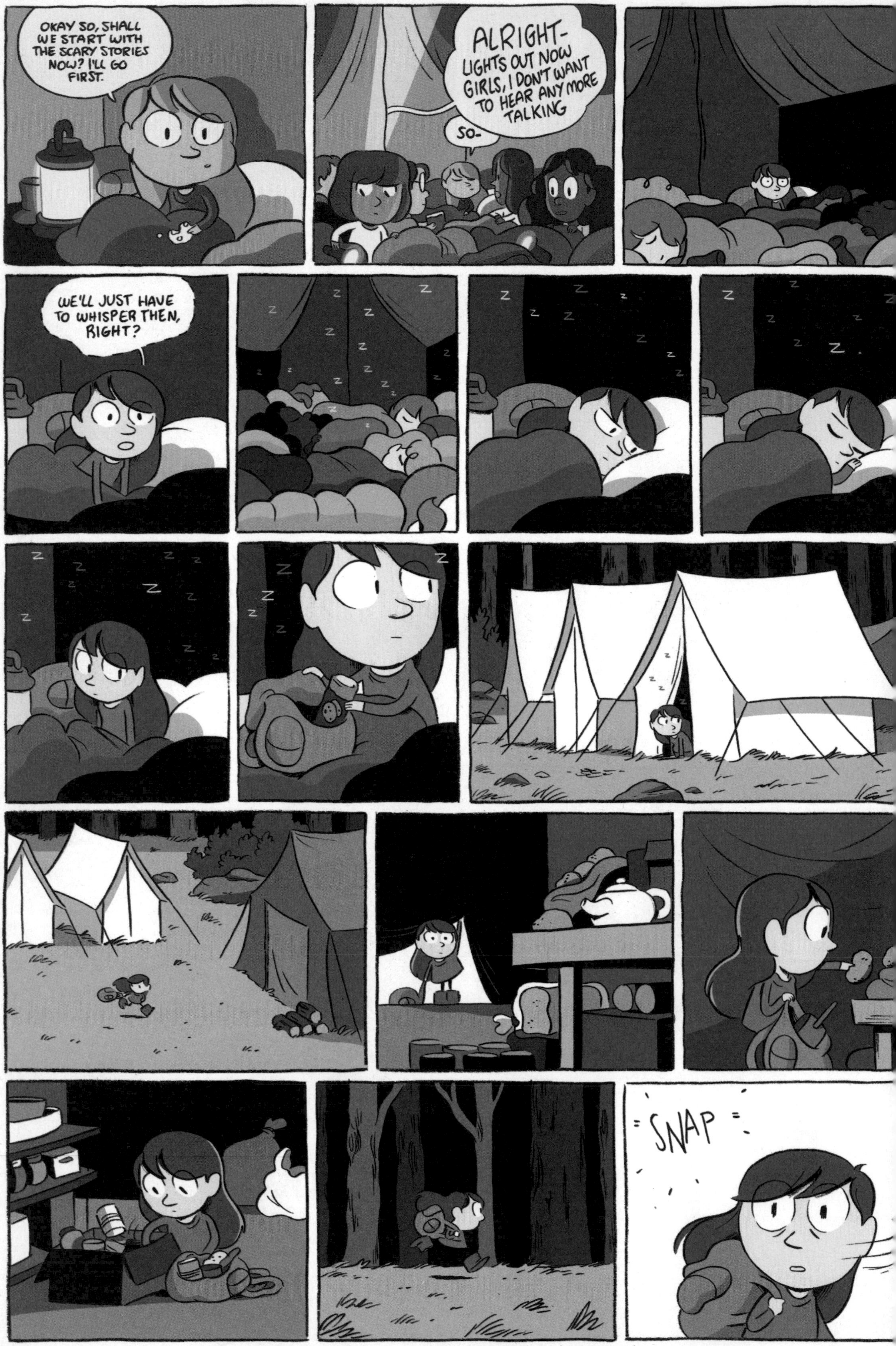
OKAY SO, SHALL WE START WITH THE SCARY STORIES NOW? I'LL GO FIRST.
ALRIGHT- LIGHTS OUT NOW GIRLS, I DON'T WANT TO HEAR ANY MORE TALKING
SO-
WE'LL JUST HAVE TO WHISPER THEN, RIGHT?
SNAP

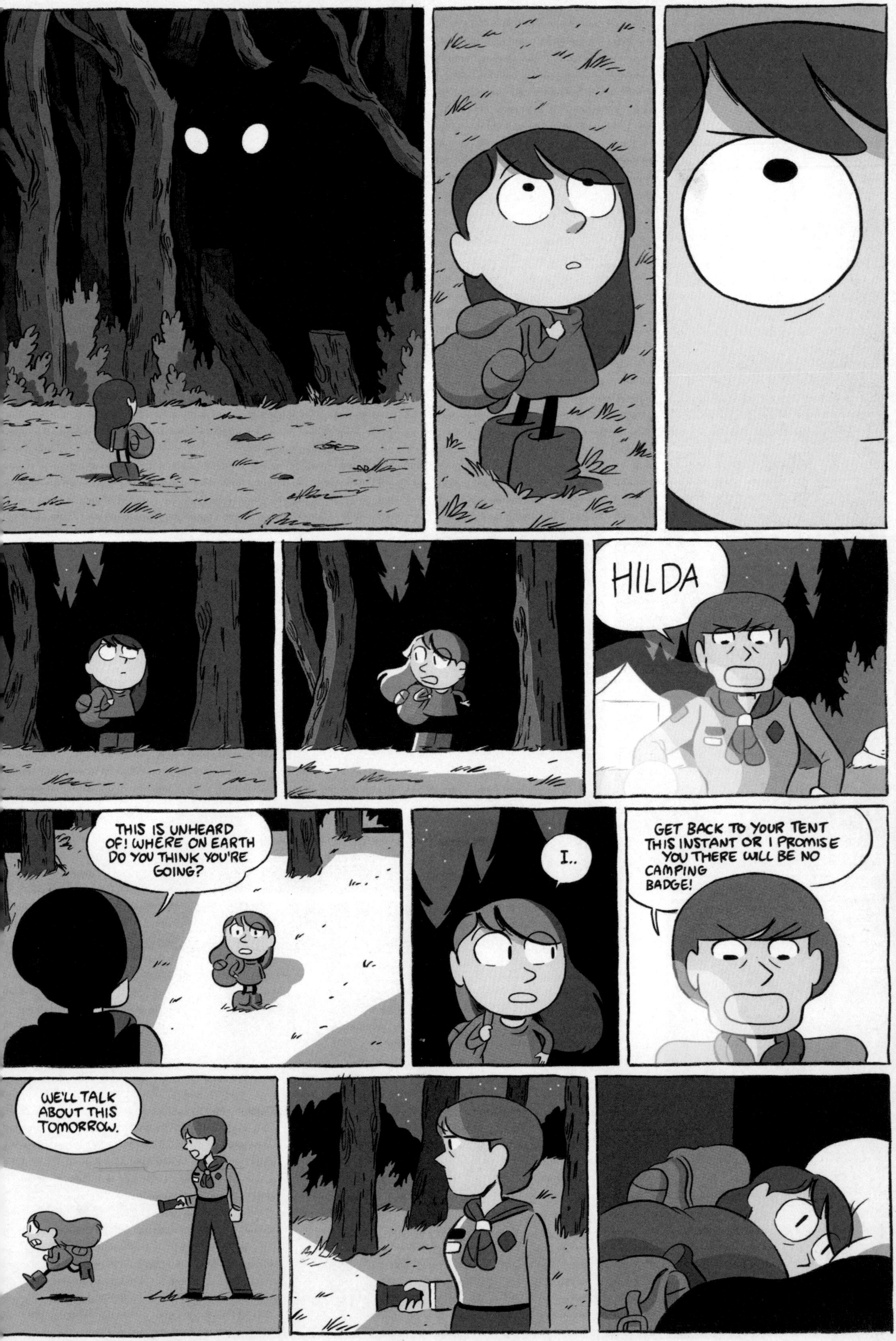
HILDA
THIS IS UNHEARD OF! WHERE ON EARTH DO YOU THINK YOU'RE GOING?
I..
GET BACK TO YOUR TENT THIS INSTANT OR I PROMISE YOU THERE WILL BE NO CAMPING BADGE!
WE'LL TALK ABOUT THIS TOMORROW.

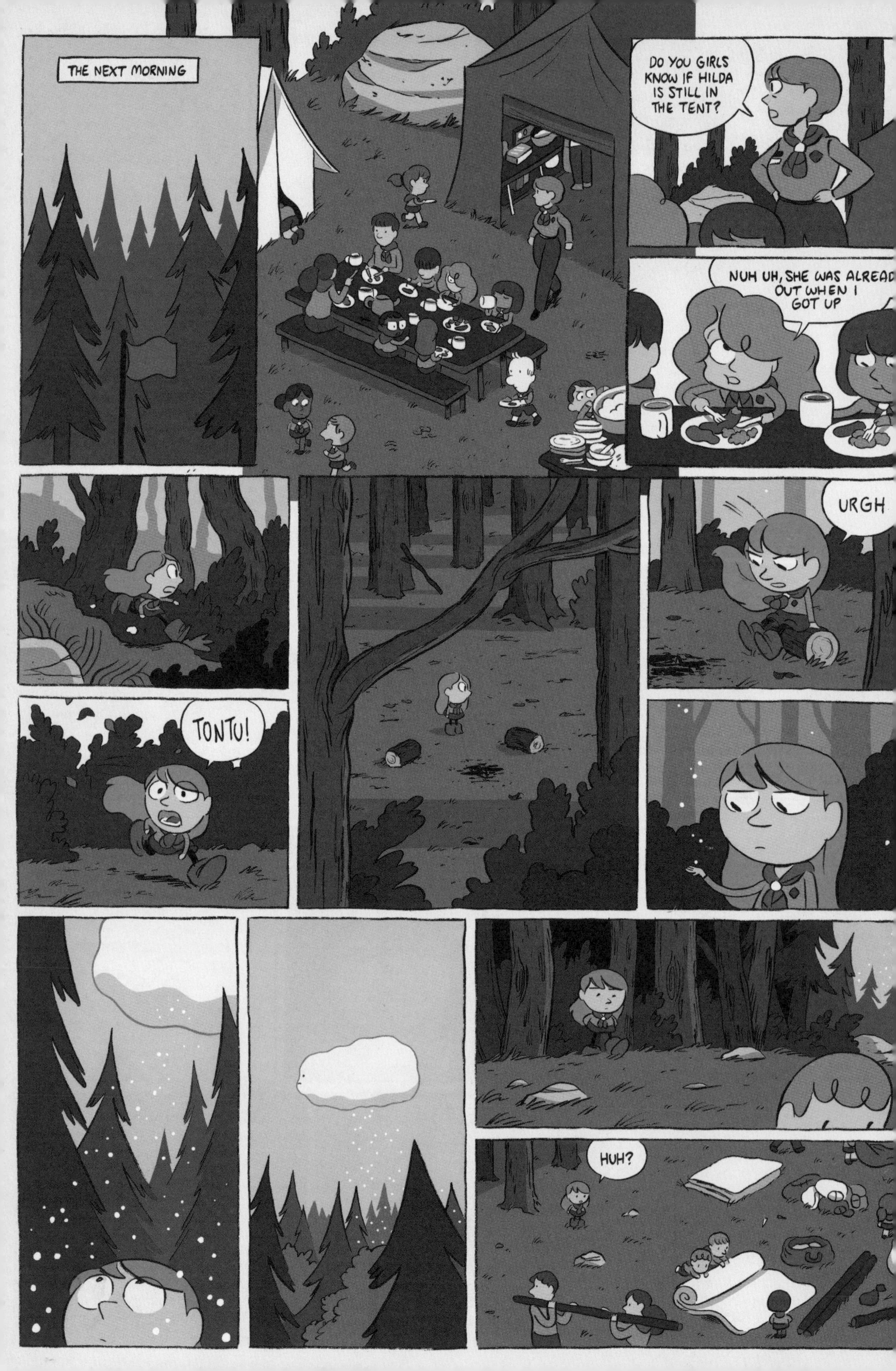
THE NEXT MORNING
DO YOU GIRLS KNOW IF HILDA IS STILL IN THE TENT?
NUH UH, SHE WAS ALREAD OUT WHEN I GOT UP
URGH
TONTU!
HUH?

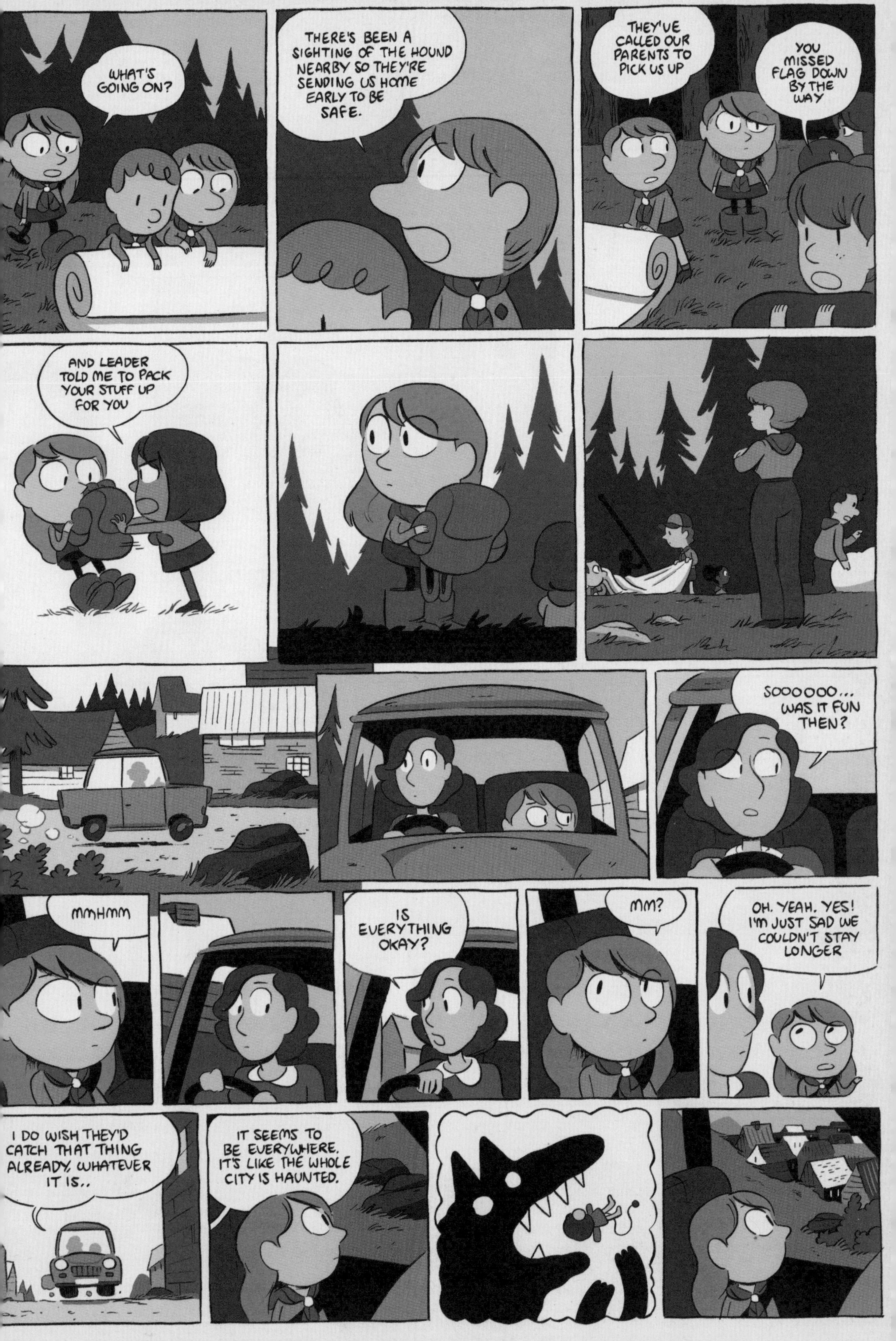
WHAT'S GOING ON?
THERE'S BEEN A SIGHTING OF THE HOUND NEARBY SO THEY'RE SENDING US HOME EARLY TO BE SAFE.
THEY'VE CALLED OUR PARENTS TO PICK US UP
YOU MISSED FLAG DOWN BY THE WAY
AND LEADER TOLD ME TO PACK YOUR STUFF UP FOR YOU
SOOOOOO... WAS IT FUN THEN?
MMHMM
IS EVERYTHING OKAY?
MM?
OH. YEAH. YES! I'M JUST SAD WE COULDN'T STAY LONGER
I DO WISH THEY'D CATCH THAT THING ALREADY, WHATEVER IT IS..
IT SEEMS TO BE EVERYWHERE. IT'S LIKE THE WHOLE CITY IS HAUNTED.

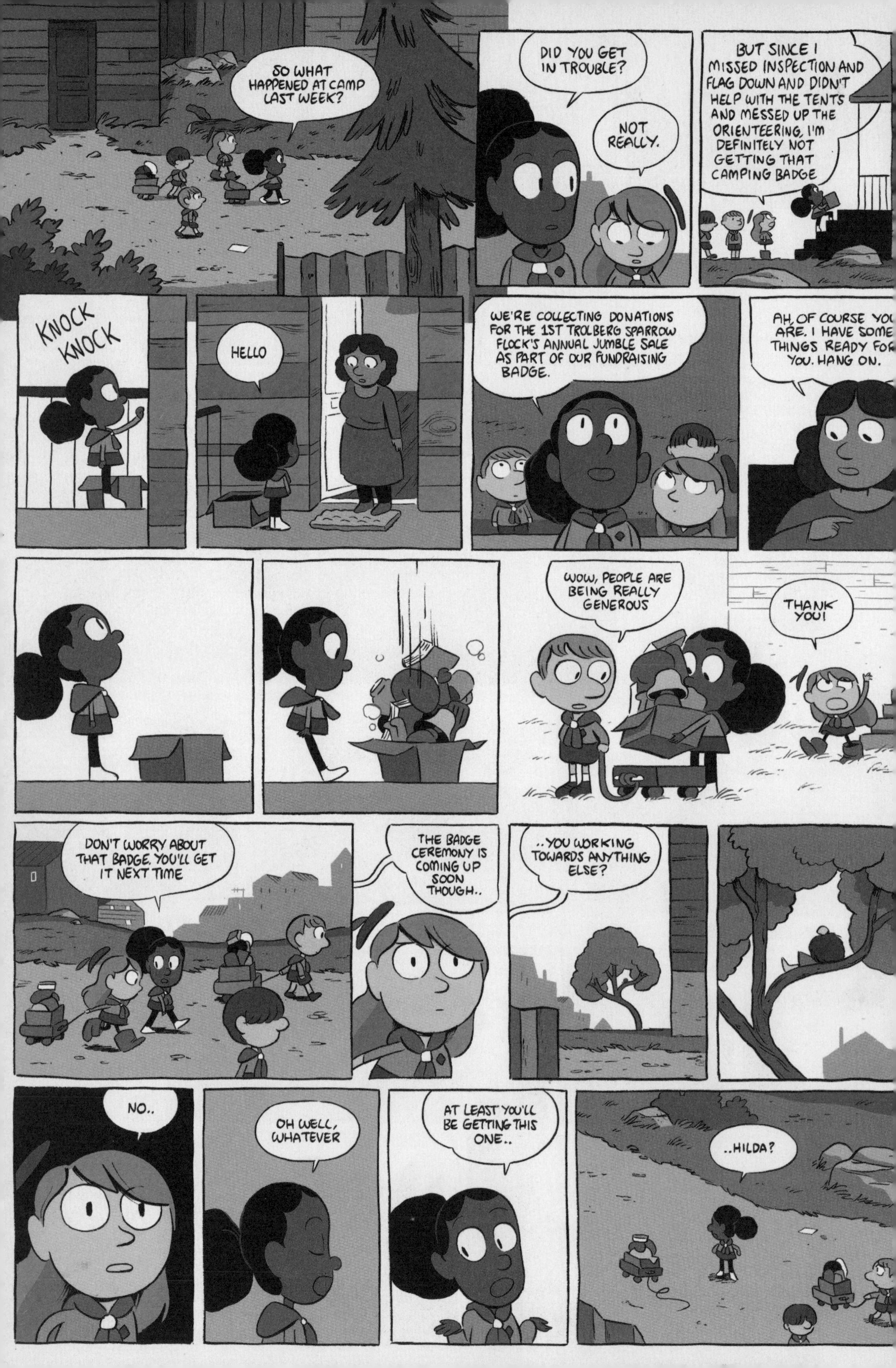
SO WHAT HAPPENED AT CAMP LAST WEEK?
DID YOU GET IN TROUBLE?
NOT REALLY.
BUT SINCE I MISSED INSPECTION AND FLAG DOWN AND DIDN'T HELP WITH THE TENTS AND MESSED UP THE ORIENTEERING, I'M DEFINITELY NOT GETTING THAT CAMPING BADGE
KNOCK KNOCK
HELLO
WE'RE COLLECTING DONATIONS FOR THE 1ST TROLBERG SPARROW FLOCK'S ANNUAL JUMBLE SALE AS PART OF OUR FUNDRAISING BADGE.
AH, OF COURSE YOU ARE. I HAVE SOME THINGS READY FOR YOU. HANG ON.
WOW, PEOPLE ARE BEING REALLY GENEROUS
THANK YOU!
DON'T WORRY ABOUT THAT BADGE. YOU'LL GET IT NEXT TIME
THE BADGE CEREMONY IS COMING UP SOON THOUGH..
..YOU WORKING TOWARDS ANYTHING ELSE?
NO..
OH WELL, WHATEVER
AT LEAST YOU'LL BE GETTING THIS ONE..
..HILDA?

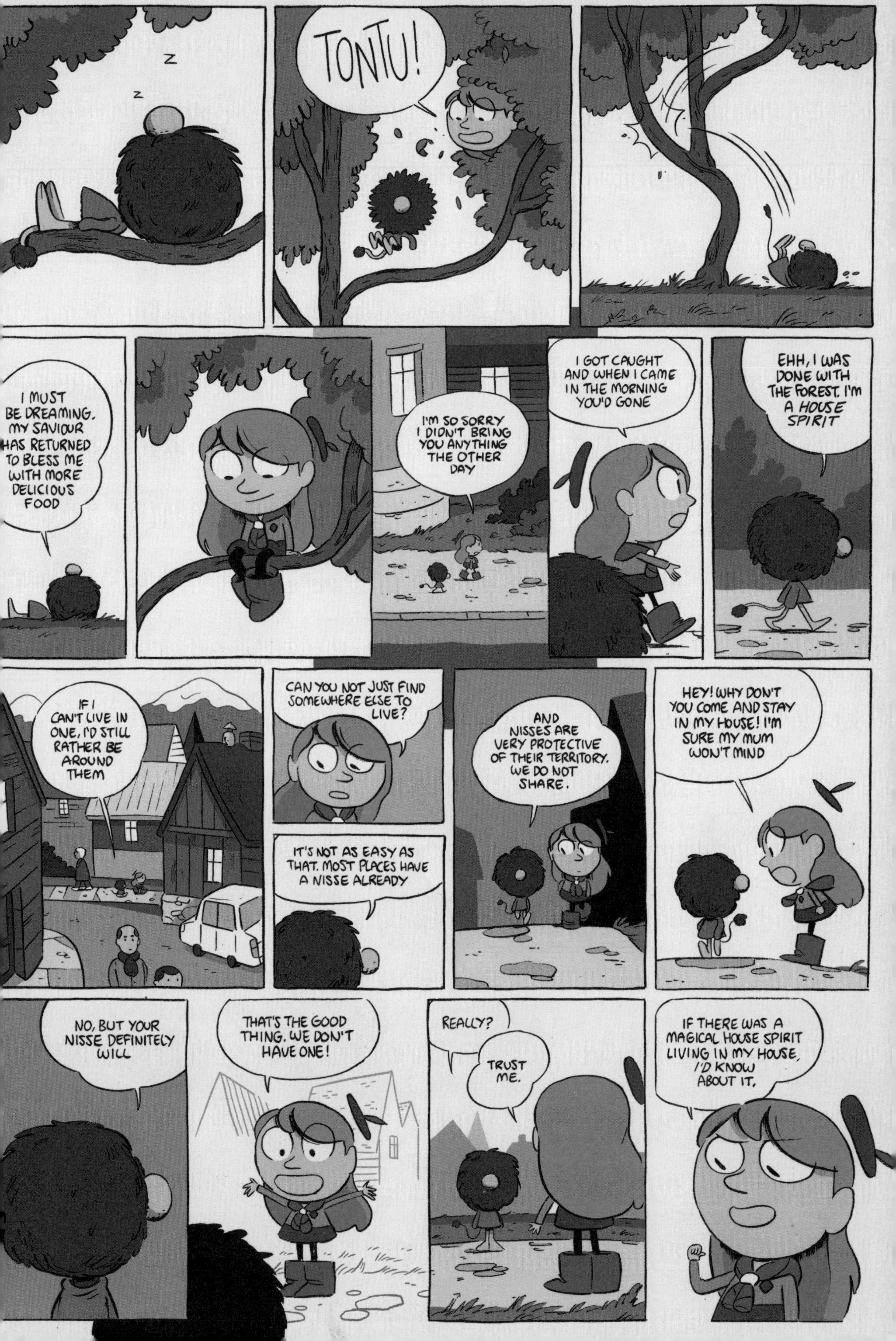
Z
Z
TONTU!
I MUST BE DREAMING. MY SAVIOUR HAS RETURNED TO BLESS ME WITH MORE DELICIOUS FOOD
I'M SO SORRY I DIDN'T BRING YOU ANYTHING THE OTHER DAY
I GOT CAUGHT AND WHEN I CAME IN THE MORNING YOU'D GONE
EHH, I WAS DONE WITH THE FOREST. I'M A HOUSE SPIRIT
IF I CAN'T LIVE IN ONE, I'D STILL RATHER BE AROUND THEM
CAN YOU NOT JUST FIND SOMEWHERE ELSE TO LIVE?
IT'S NOT AS EASY AS THAT. MOST PLACES HAVE A NISSE ALREADY
AND NISSES ARE VERY PROTECTIVE OF THEIR TERRITORY. WE DO NOT SHARE.
HEY! WHY DON'T YOU COME AND STAY IN MY HOUSE! I'M SURE MY MUM WON'T MIND
NO, BUT YOUR NISSE DEFINITELY WILL
THAT'S THE GOOD THING. WE DON'T HAVE ONE!
REALLY?
TRUST ME.
IF THERE WAS A MAGICAL HOUSE SPIRIT LIVING IN MY HOUSE, I'D KNOW ABOUT IT.

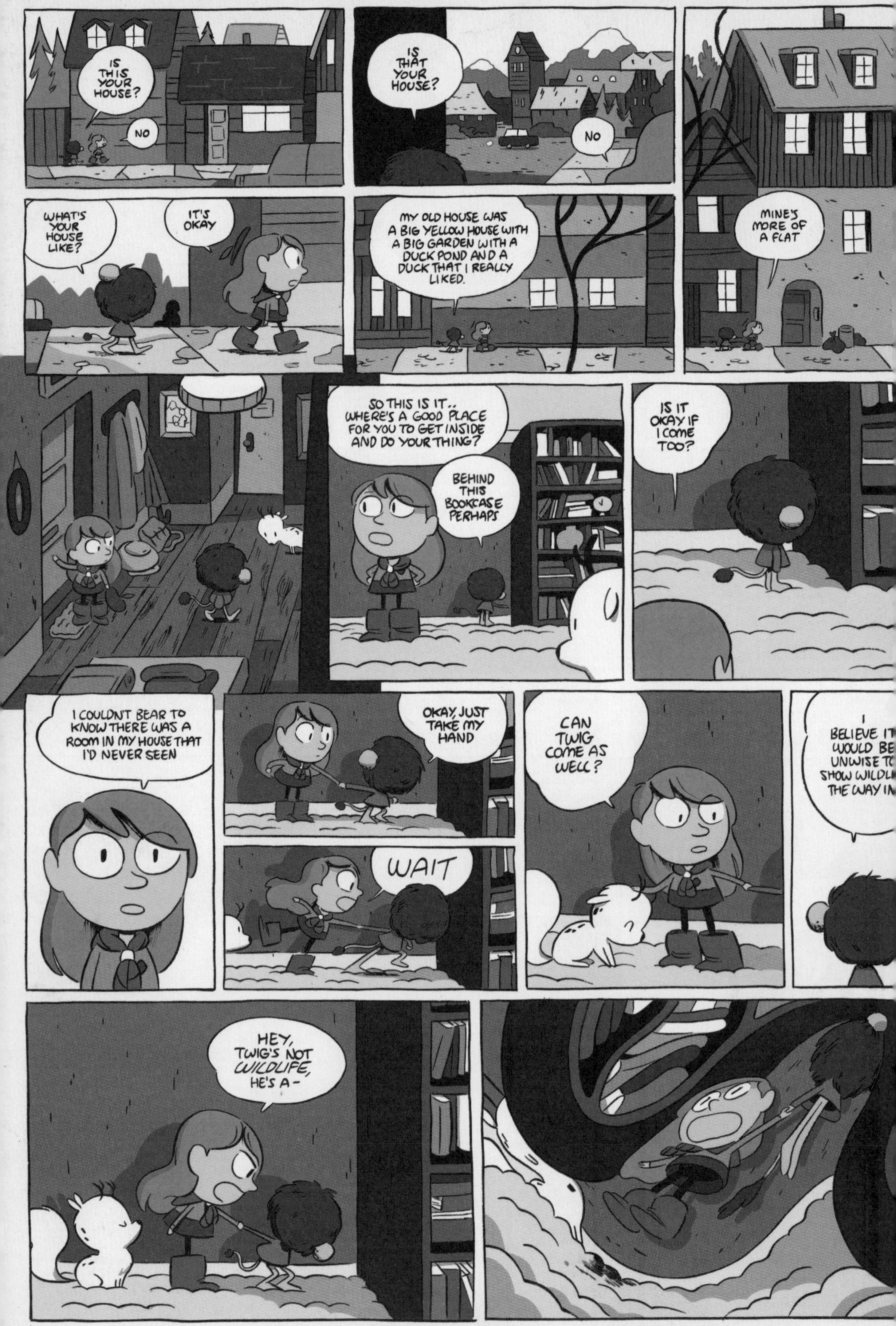
IS THIS YOUR HOUSE?
NO
IS THAT YOUR HOUSE?
NO
WHAT'S YOUR HOUSE LIKE?
IT'S OKAY
MY OLD HOUSE WAS A BIG YELLOW HOUSE WITH A BIG GARDEN WITH A DUCK POND AND A DUCK THAT I REALLY LIKED.
MINE'S MORE OF A FLAT
SO THIS IS IT.. WHERE'S A GOOD PLACE FOR YOU TO GET INSIDE AND DO YOUR THING?
BEHIND THIS BOOKCASE PERHAPS
IS IT OKAY IF I COME TOO?
I COULDN'T BEAR TO KNOW THERE WAS A ROOM IN MY HOUSE THAT I'D NEVER SEEN
OKAY, JUST TAKE MY HAND
WAIT
CAN TWIG COME AS WELL?
HEY, TWIG'S NOT WILDLIFE, HE'S A-

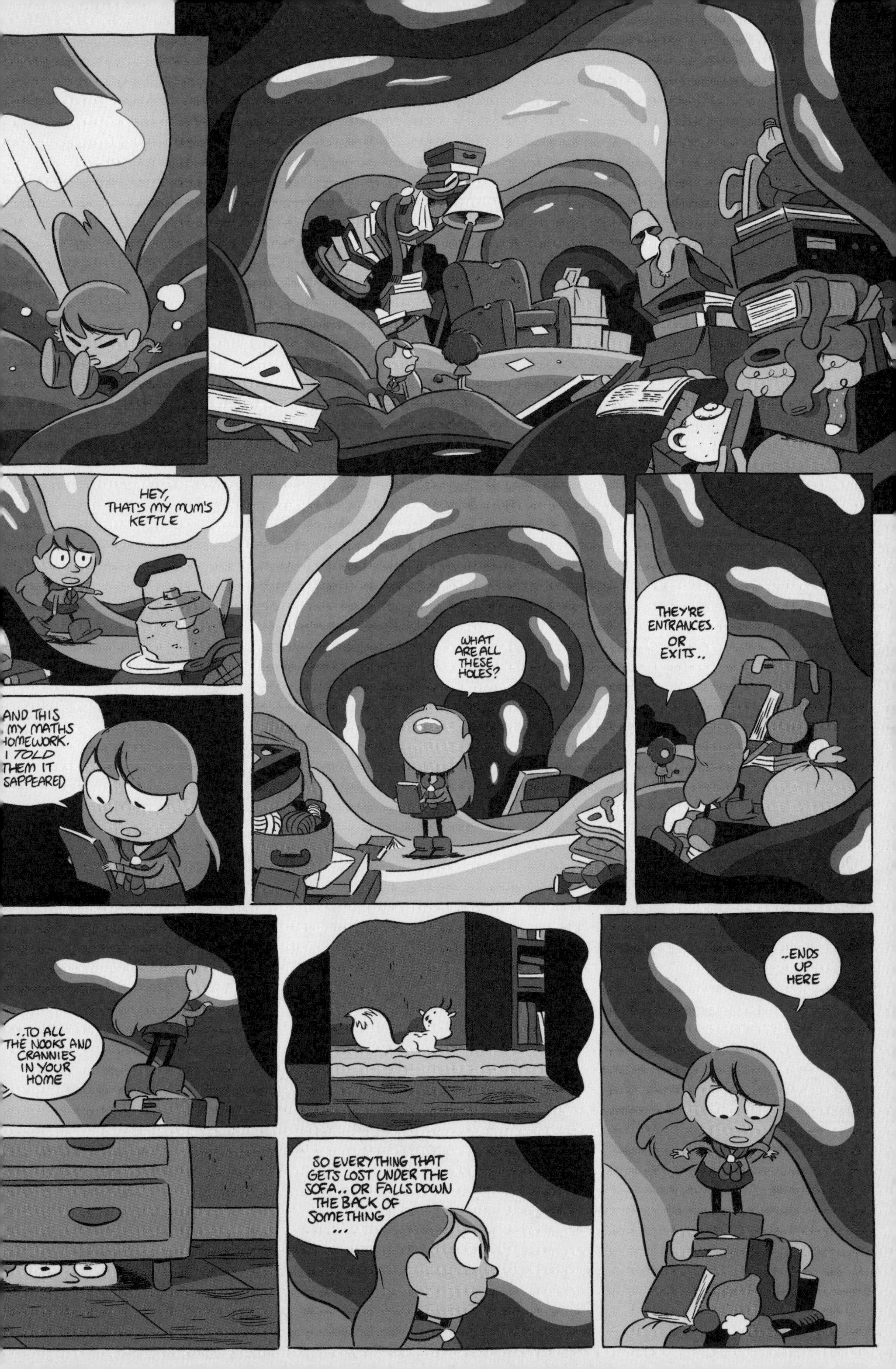
HEY, THAT'S MY MUM'S KETTLE
AND THIS MY MATHS HOMEWORK. I TOLD THEM IT SAPPEARED
WHAT ARE ALL THESE HOLES?
THEY'RE ENTRANCES. OR EXITS..
..TO ALL THE NOOKS AND CRANNIES IN YOUR HOME
SO EVERYTHING THAT GETS LOST UNDER THE SOFA.. OR FALLS DOWN THE BACK OF SOMETHING ...
..ENDS UP HERE

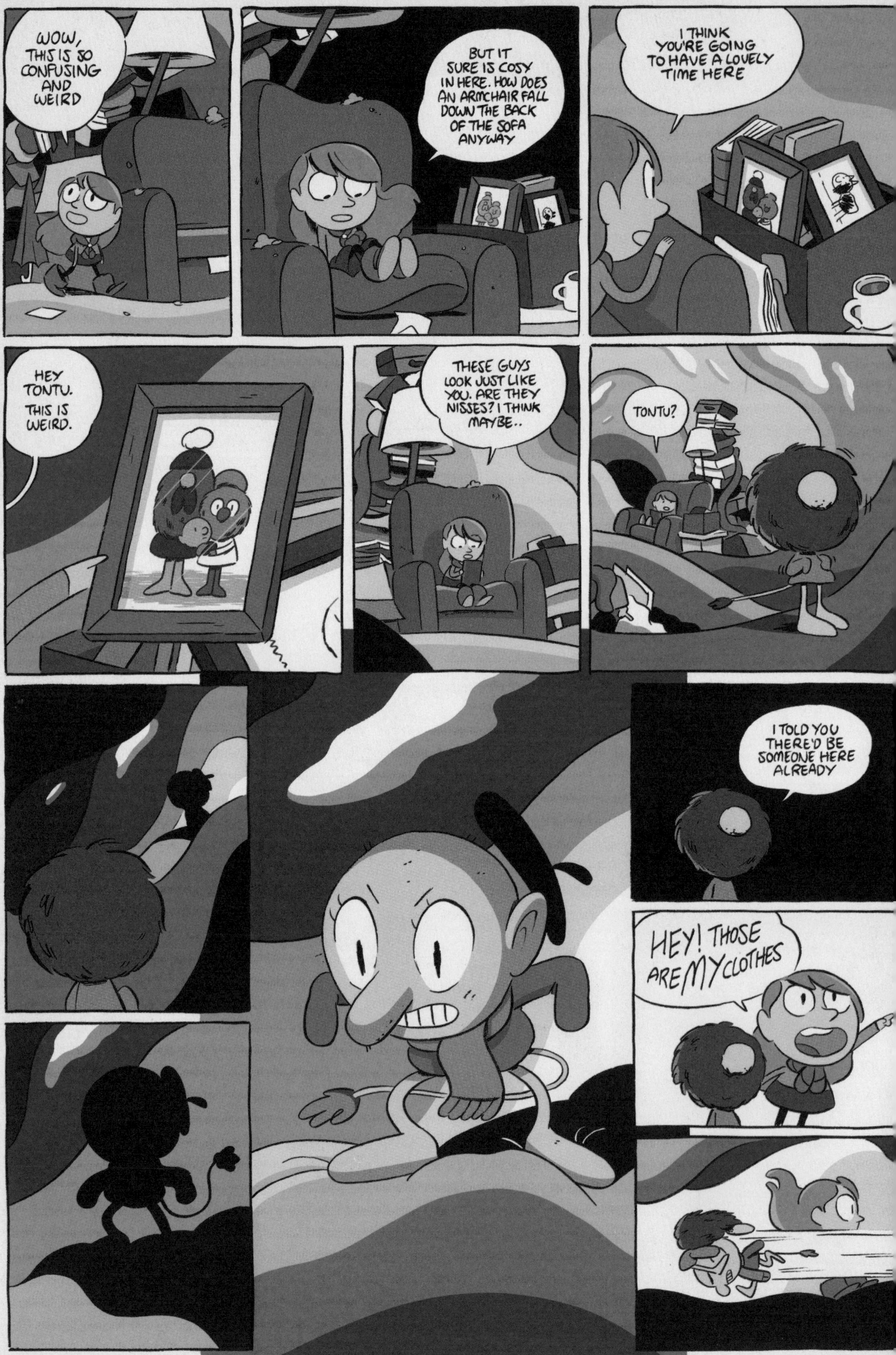
WOW, THIS IS SO CONFUSING AND WEIRD
BUT IT SURE IS COSY IN HERE. HOW DOES AN ARMCHAIR FALL DOWN THE BACK OF THE SOFA ANYWAY
I THINK YOU'RE GOING TO HAVE A LOVELY TIME HERE
HEY TONTU. THIS IS WEIRD.
THESE GUYS LOOK JUST LIKE YOU. ARE THEY NISSES? I THINK MAYBE..
TONTU?
I TOLD YOU THERE'D BE SOMEONE HERE ALREADY
HEY! THOSE ARE MY CLOTHES

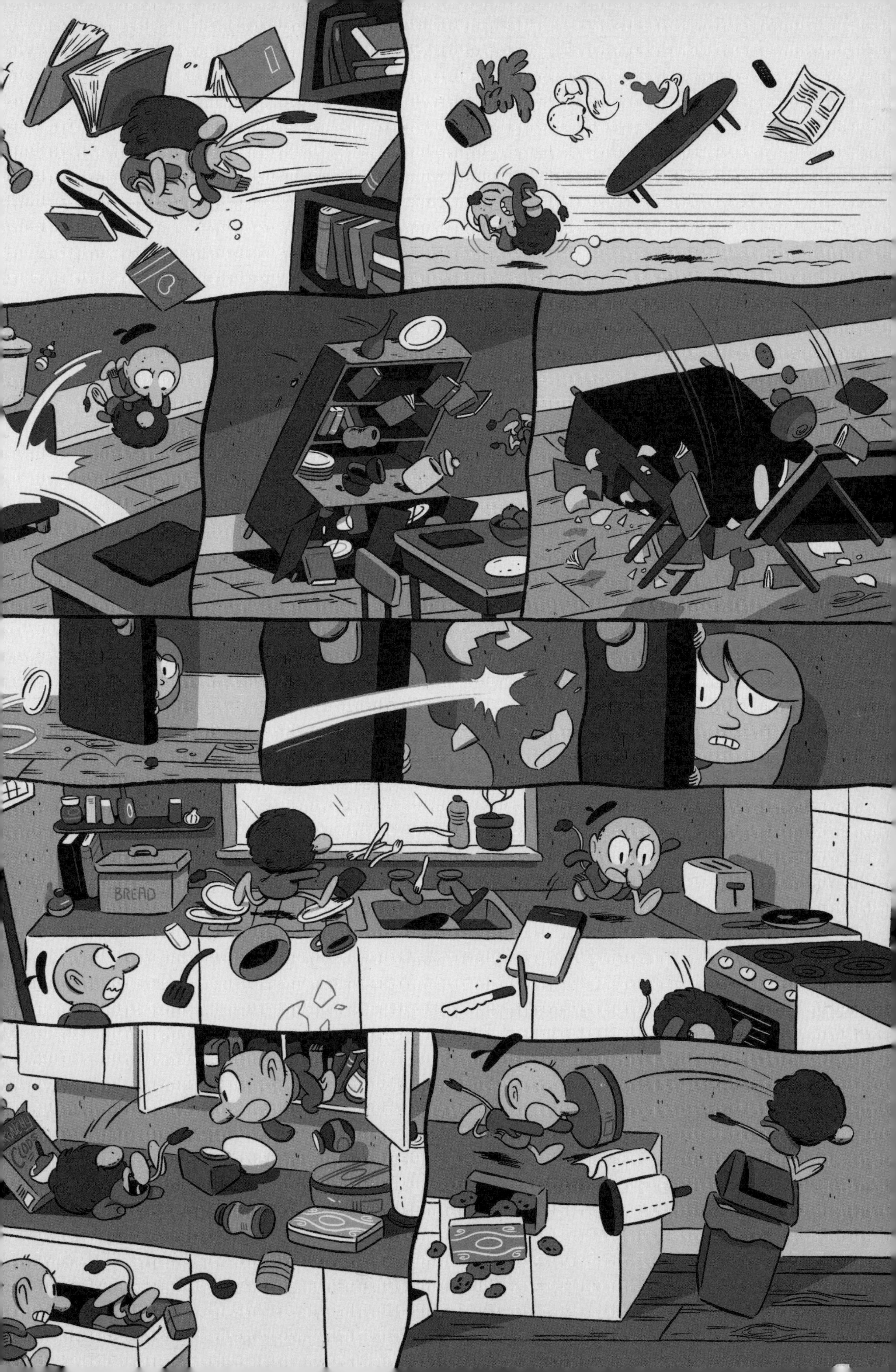
BREAD
CLODS

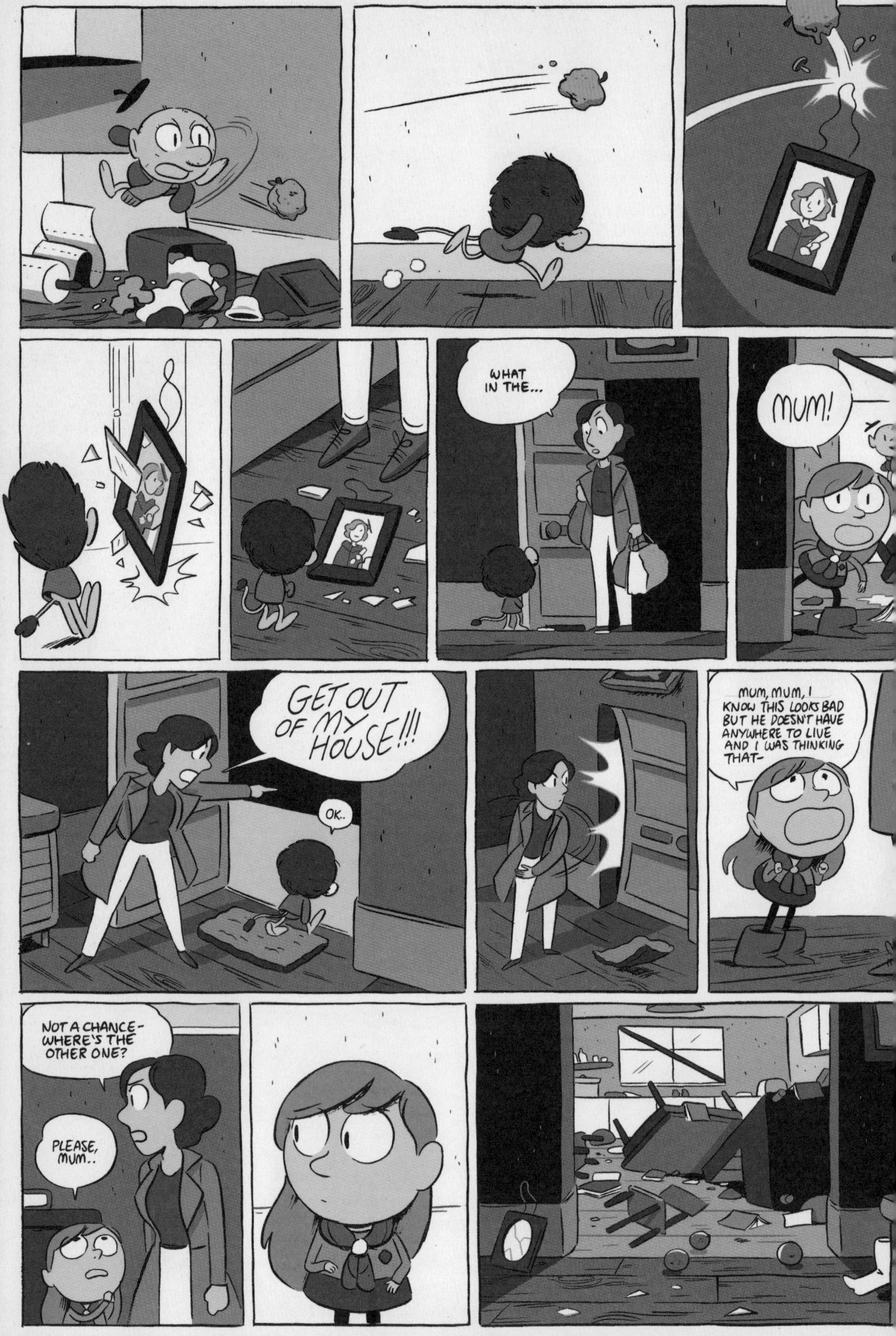
WHAT IN THE...
MUM!
GET OUT OF MY HOUSE!!!
OK..
MUM, MUM, I KNOW THIS LOOKS BAD BUT HE DOESN'T HAVE ANYWHERE TO LIVE AND I WAS THINKING THAT-
NOT A CHANCE- WHERE'S THE OTHER ONE?
PLEASE, MUM..

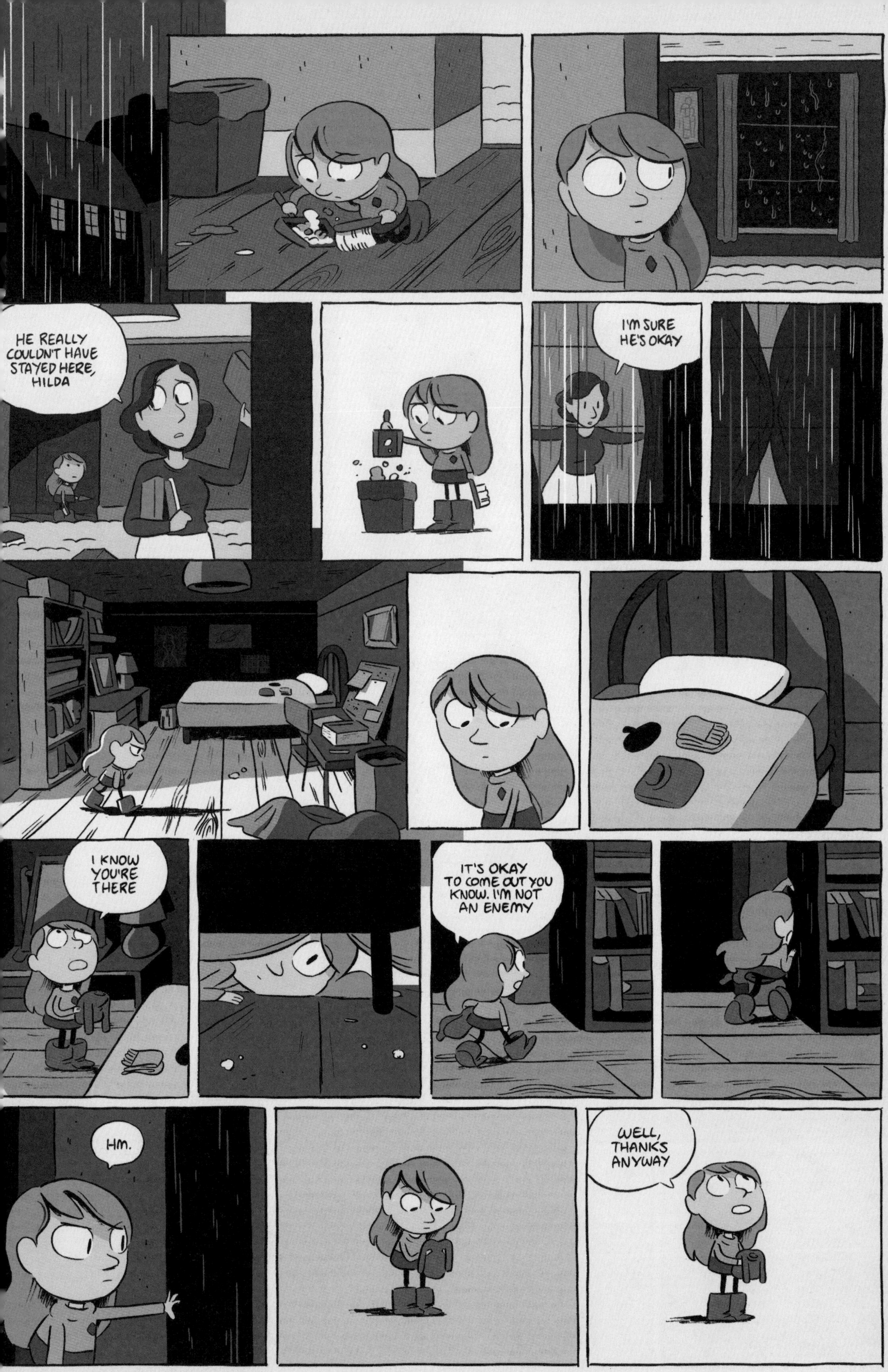
HE REALLY COULDN'T HAVE STAYED HERE, HILDA
I'M SURE HE'S OKAY
I KNOW YOU'RE THERE
IT'S OKAY TO COME OUT YOU KNOW. I'M NOT AN ENEMY
HM.
WELL, THANKS ANYWAY

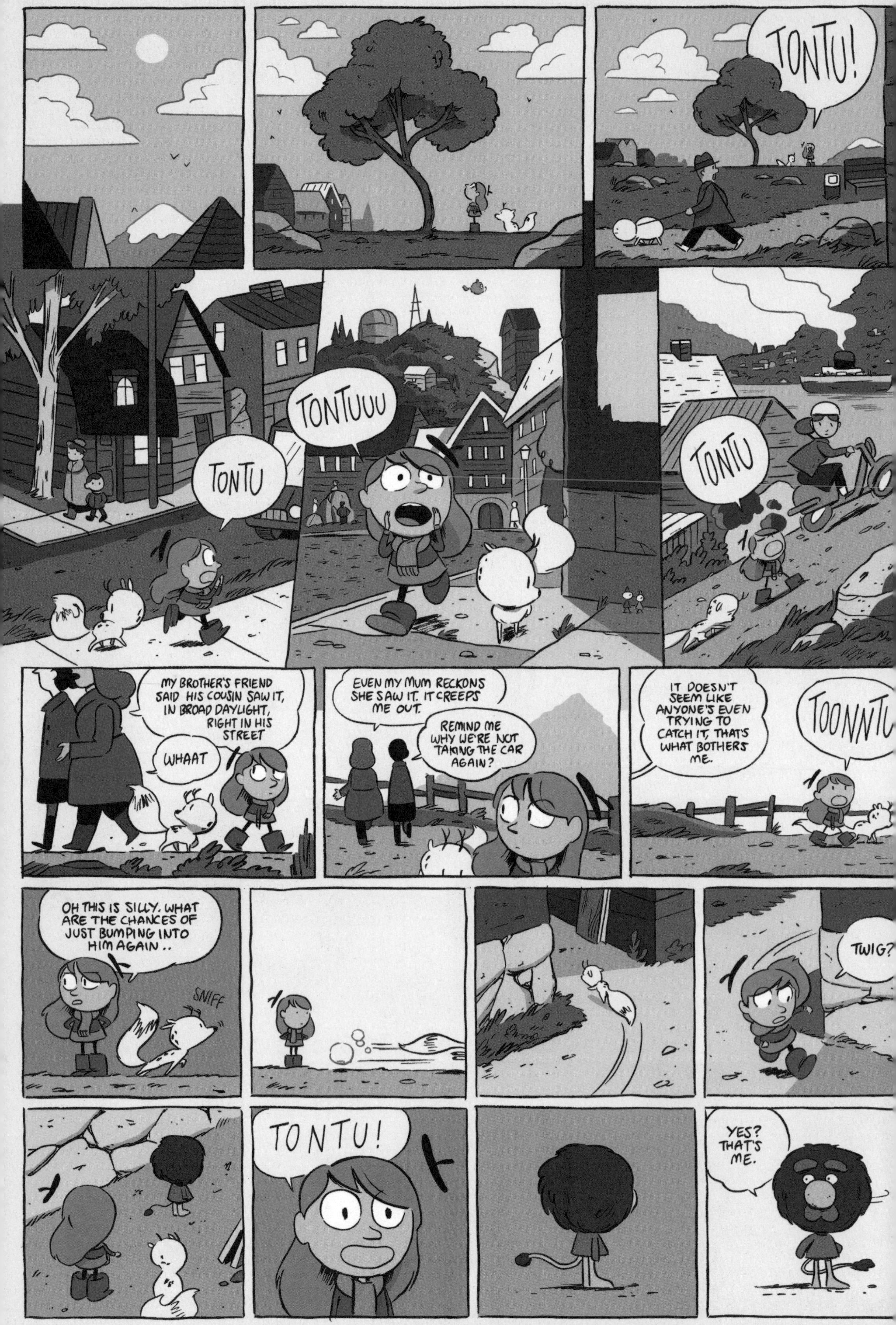
TONTU!
TONTU
TONTUUU
TONTU
MY BROTHER'S FRIEND SAID HIS COUSIN SAW IT, IN BROAD DAYLIGHT, RIGHT IN HIS STREET
WHAAT
EVEN MY MUM RECKONS SHE SAW IT. IT CREEPS ME OUT.
REMIND ME WHY WE'RE NOT TAKING THE CAR AGAIN?
IT DOESN'T SEEM LIKE ANYONE'S EVEN TRYING TO CATCH IT, THAT'S WHAT BOTHERS ME.
TOONNTU
OH THIS IS SILLY. WHAT ARE THE CHANCES OF JUST BUMPING INTO HIM AGAIN..
SNIFF
TWIG?
TONTU!
YES? THAT'S ME.

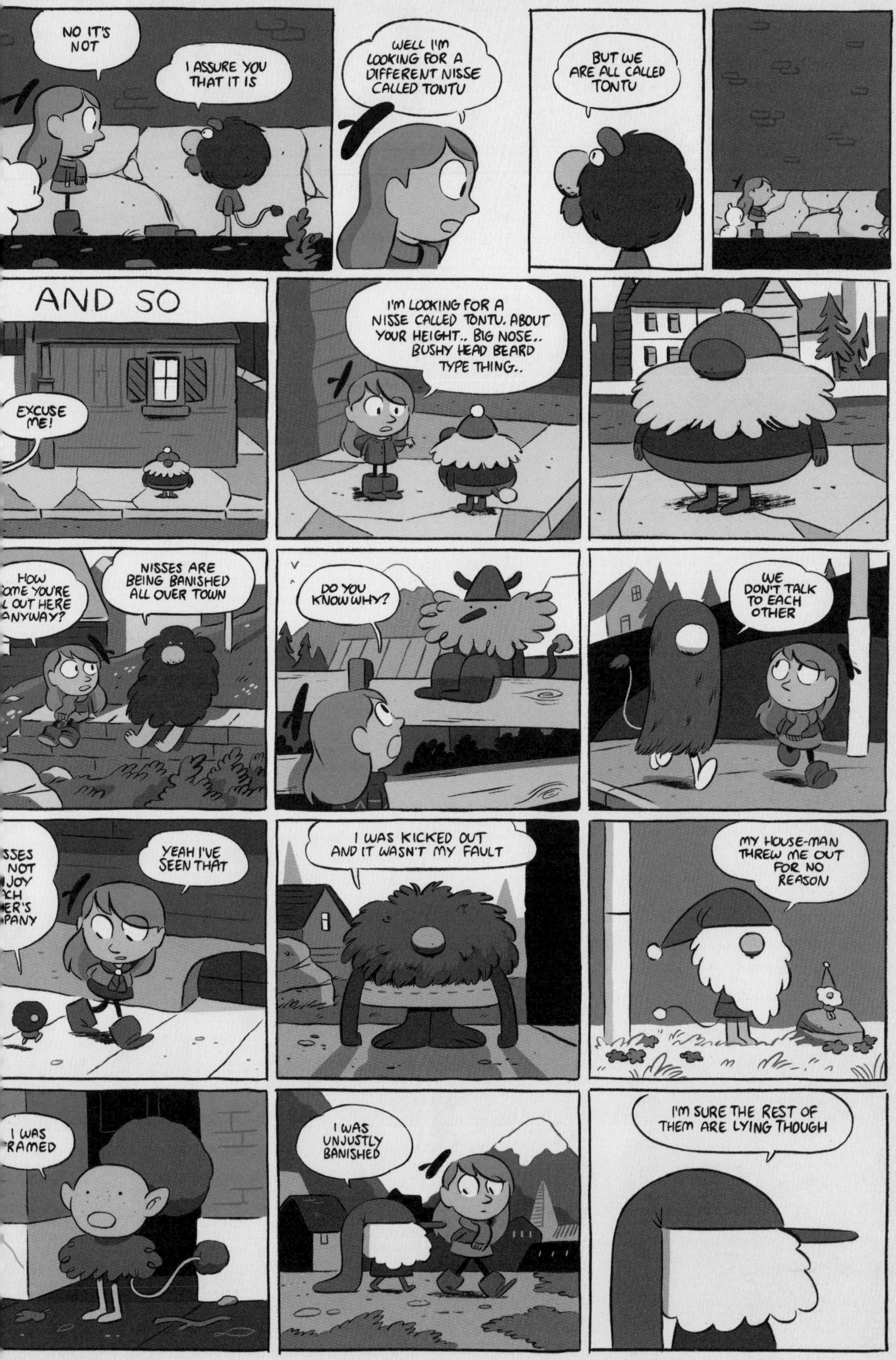

NO IT'S NOT
I ASSURE YOU THAT IT IS
WELL I'M LOOKING FOR A DIFFERENT NISSE CALLED TONTU
BUT WE ARE ALL CALLED TONTU
AND SO
EXCUSE ME!
I'M LOOKING FOR A NISSE CALLED TONTU. ABOUT YOUR HEIGHT.. BIG NOSE.. BUSHY HEAD BEARD TYPE THING..
HOW OME YOU'RE L OUT HERE ANYWAY?
NISSES ARE BEING BANISHED ALL OVER TOWN
DO YOU KNOW WHY?
WE DON'T TALK TO EACH OTHER
SSES NOT JOY CH ER'S PANY
YEAH I'VE SEEN THAT
I WAS KICKED OUT AND IT WASN'T MY FAULT
MY HOUSE-MAN THREW ME OUT FOR NO REASON
I WAS RAMED
I WAS UNJUSTLY BANISHED
I'M SURE THE REST OF THEM ARE LYING THOUGH

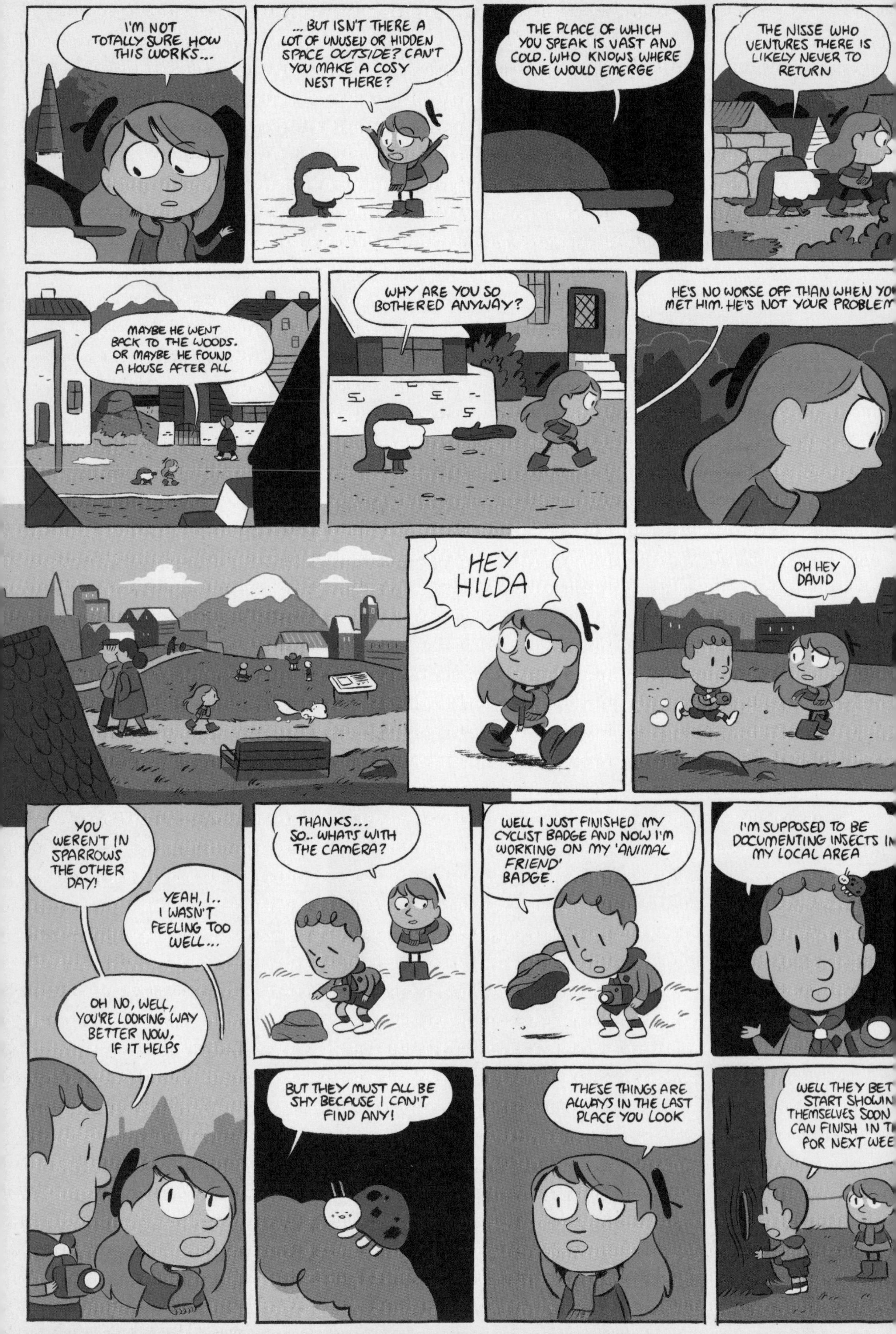
I'M NOT TOTALLY SURE HOW THIS WORKS...
... BUT ISN'T THERE A LOT OF UNUSED OR HIDDEN SPACE OUTSIDE? CAN'T YOU MAKE A COSY NEST THERE?
THE PLACE OF WHICH YOU SPEAK IS VAST AND COLD. WHO KNOWS WHERE ONE WOULD EMERGE
THE NISSE WHO VENTURES THERE IS LIKELY NEVER TO RETURN
MAYBE HE WENT BACK TO THE WOODS. OR MAYBE HE FOUND A HOUSE AFTER ALL
WHY ARE YOU SO BOTHERED ANYWAY?
HE'S NO WORSE OFF THAN WHEN YO
MET HIM. HE'S NOT YOUR PROBLEM
HEY HILDA
OH HEY DAVID
YOU WEREN'T IN SPARROWS THE OTHER DAY!
YEAH, I.. I WASN'T FEELING TOO WELL...
OH NO, WELL, YOU'RE LOOKING WAY BETTER NOW, IF IT HELPS
THANKS... SO.. WHATS WITH THE CAMERA?
WELL I JUST FINISHED MY CYCLIST BADGE AND NOW I'M WORKING ON MY 'ANIMAL FRIEND' BADGE.
I'M SUPPOSED TO BE DOCUMENTING INSECTS IN MY LOCAL AREA
BUT THEY MUST ALL BE SHY BECAUSE I CAN'T FIND ANY!
THESE THINGS ARE ALWAYS IN THE LAST PLACE YOU LOOK
WELL THEY BET START SHOWIN THEMSELVES SOON CAN FINISH IN T FOR NEXT WEE

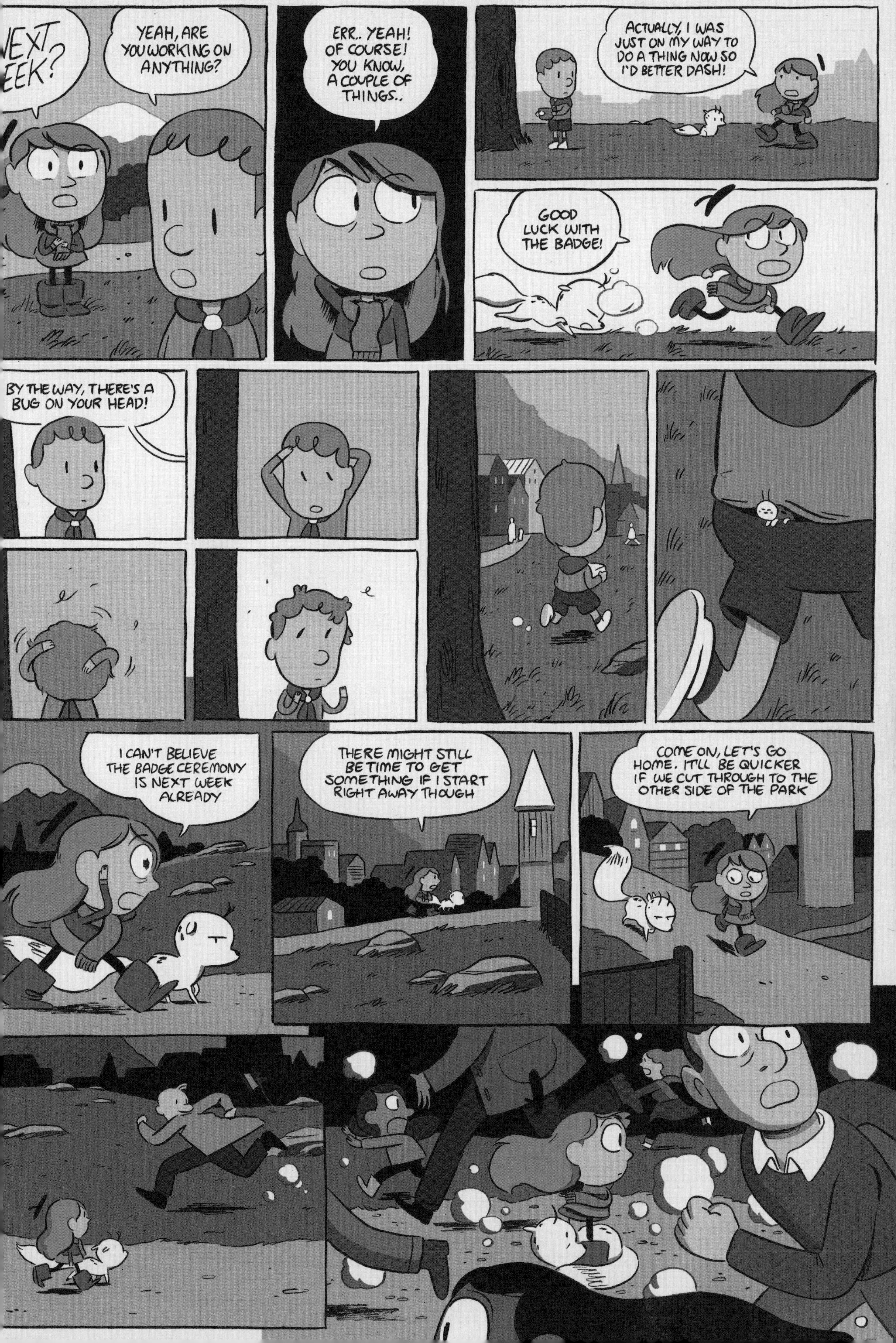
NEXT WEEK?
YEAH, ARE YOU WORKING ON ANYTHING?
ERR.. YEAH! OF COURSE! YOU KNOW, A COUPLE OF THINGS..
ACTUALLY, I WAS JUST ON MY WAY TO DO A THING NOW SO I'D BETTER DASH!
GOOD LUCK WITH THE BADGE!
BY THE WAY, THERE'S A BUG ON YOUR HEAD!
I CAN'T BELIEVE THE BADGE CEREMONY IS NEXT WEEK ALREADY
THERE MIGHT STILL BE TIME TO GET SOMETHING IF I START RIGHT AWAY THOUGH
COME ON, LET'S GO HOME. IT'LL BE QUICKER IF WE CUT THROUGH TO THE OTHER SIDE OF THE PARK

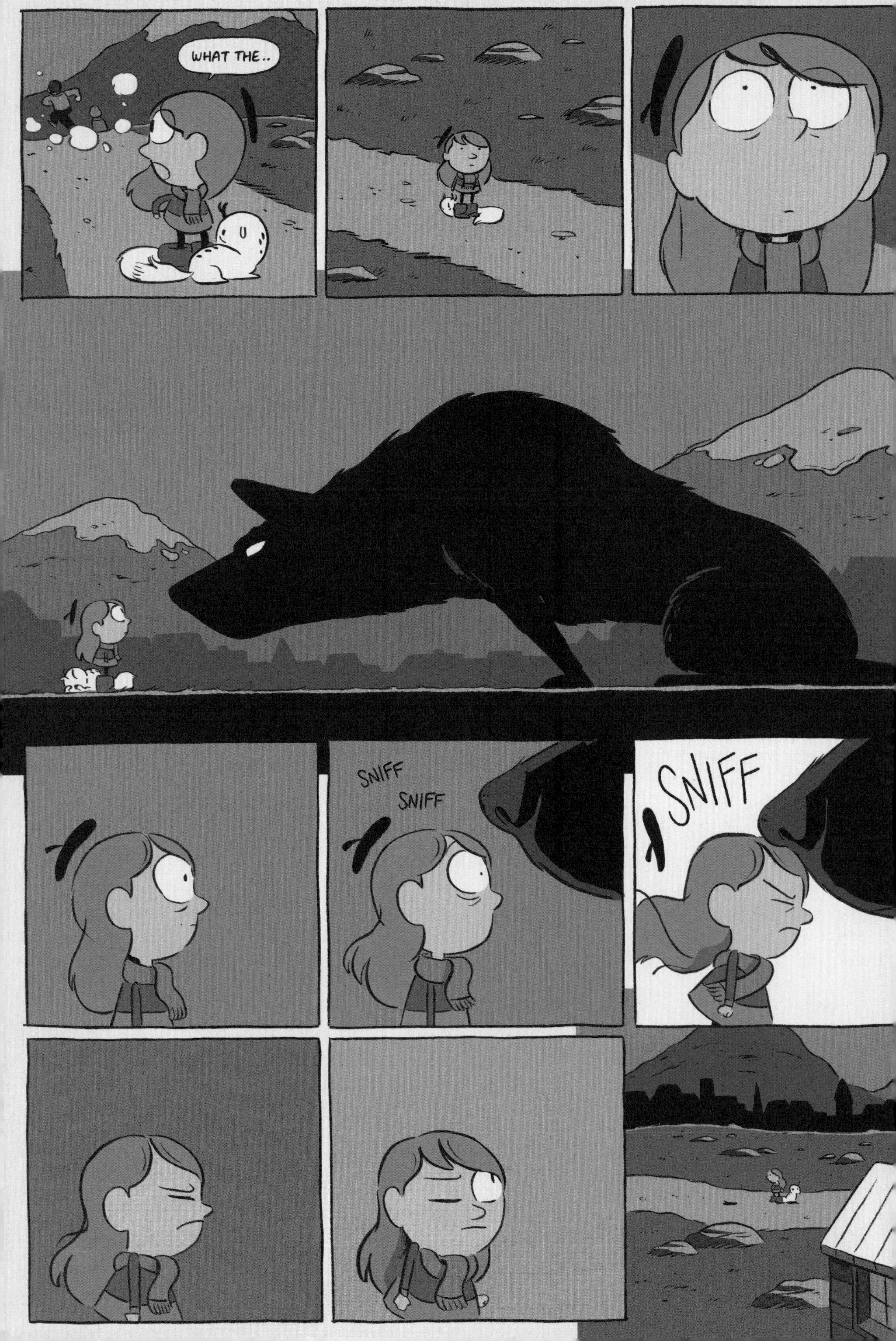
WHAT THE..
SNIFF
SNIFF
SNIFF

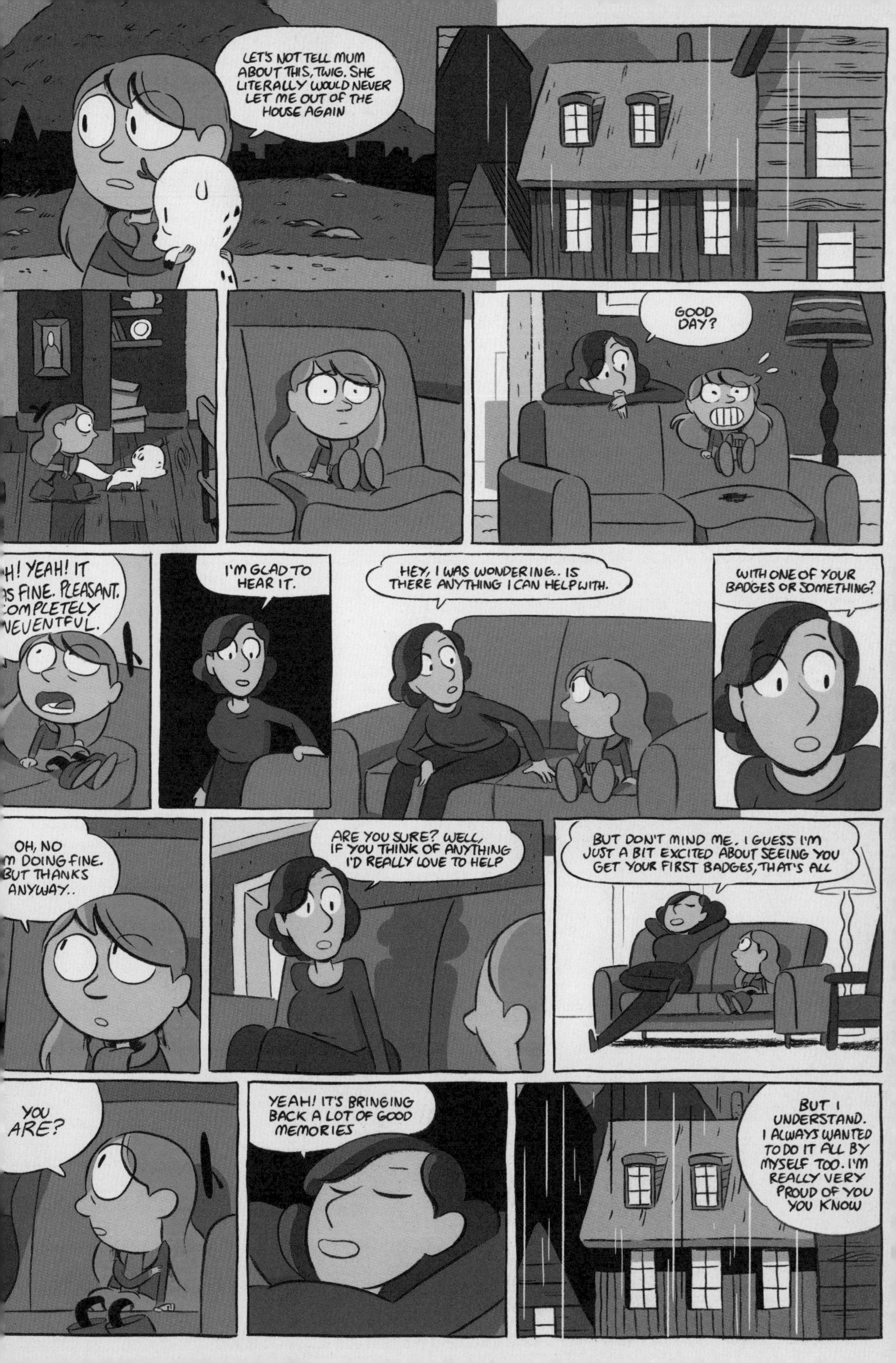
LET'S NOT TELL MUM ABOUT THIS, TWIG. SHE LITERALLY WOULD NEVER LET ME OUT OF THE HOUSE AGAIN
GOOD DAY?
H! YEAH! IT AS FINE. PLEASANT. COMPLETELY NEVENTFUL.
I'M GLAD TO HEAR IT.
HEY, I WAS WONDERING.. IS THERE ANYTHING I CAN HELP WITH.
WITH ONE OF YOUR BADGES OR SOMETHING?
OH, NO M DOING FINE. BUT THANKS ANYWAY..
ARE YOU SURE? WELL, IF YOU THINK OF ANYTHING I'D REALLY LOVE TO HELP
BUT DON'T MIND ME. I GUESS I'M JUST A BIT EXCITED ABOUT SEEING YOU GET YOUR FIRST BADGES, THAT'S ALL
YOU ARE?
YEAH! IT'S BRINGING BACK A LOT OF GOOD MEMORIES
BUT I UNDERSTAND. I ALWAYS WANTED TO DO IT ALL BY MYSELF TOO. I'M REALLY VERY PROUD OF YOU YOU KNOW

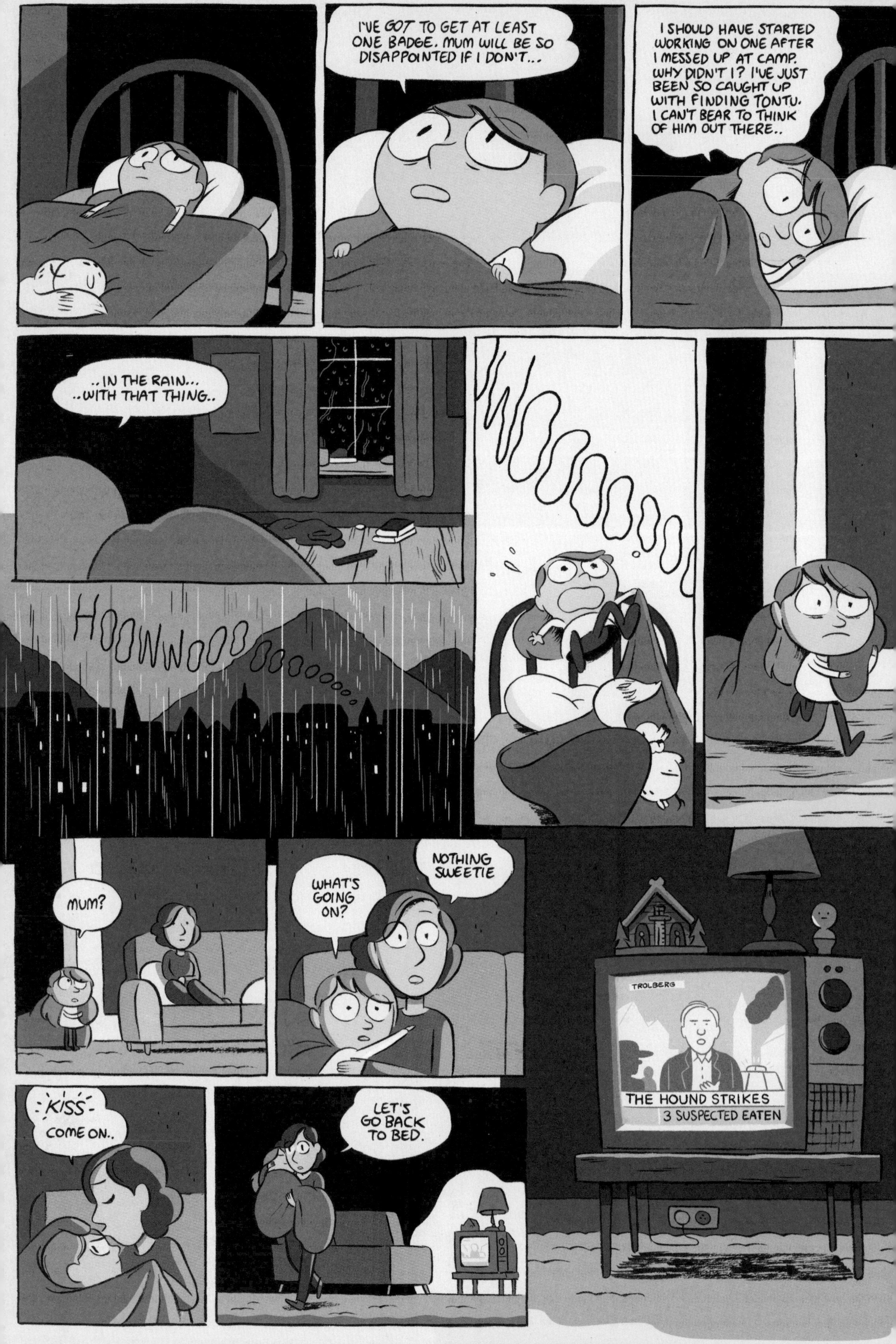
I'VE GOT TO GET AT LEAST ONE BADGE. MUM WILL BE SO DISAPPOINTED IF I DON'T...
I SHOULD HAVE STARTED WORKING ON ONE AFTER I MESSED UP AT CAMP. WHY DIDN'T I? I'VE JUST BEEN SO CAUGHT UP WITH FINDING TONTU. I CAN'T BEAR TO THINK OF HIM OUT THERE..
..IN THE RAIN... ..WITH THAT THING..
WOOOOOOOO
HOOWNWOOOOOOOOOO
MUM?
WHAT'S GOING ON?
NOTHING SWEETIE
KISS
COME ON..
LET'S GO BACK TO BED.
TROLBERG
THE HOUND STRIKES
3 SUSPECTED EATEN

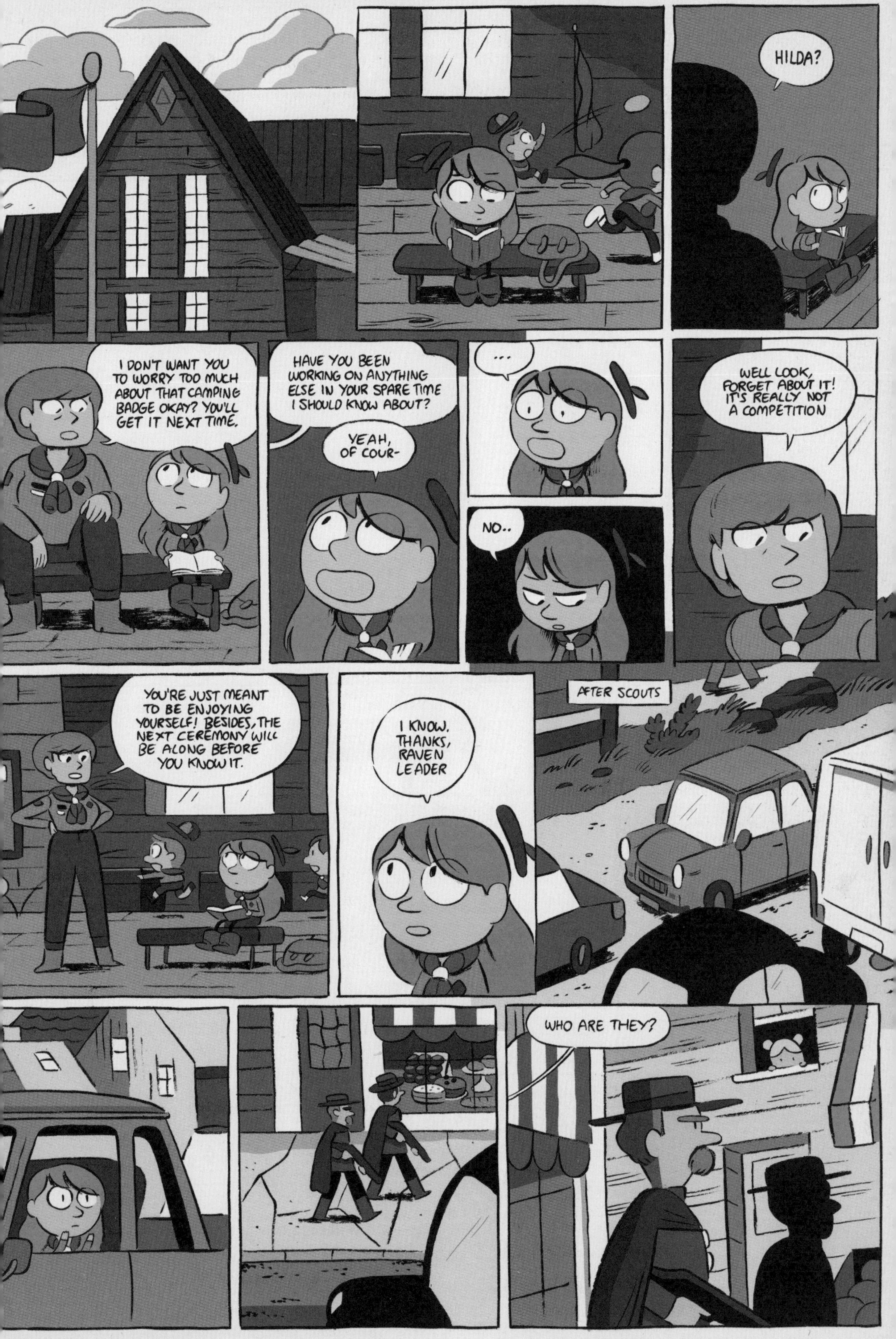
HILDA?
I DON'T WANT YOU TO WORRY TOO MUCH ABOUT THAT CAMPING BADGE OKAY? YOU'LL GET IT NEXT TIME.
HAVE YOU BEEN WORKING ON ANYTHING ELSE IN YOUR SPARE TIME I SHOULD KNOW ABOUT?
YEAH, OF COUR-
...
NO..
WELL LOOK, FORGET ABOUT IT! IT'S REALLY NOT A COMPETITION
YOU'RE JUST MEANT TO BE ENJOYING YOURSELF! BESIDES, THE NEXT CEREMONY WILL BE ALONG BEFORE YOU KNOW IT.
I KNOW. THANKS, RAVEN LEADER
AFTER SCOUTS
WHO ARE THEY?

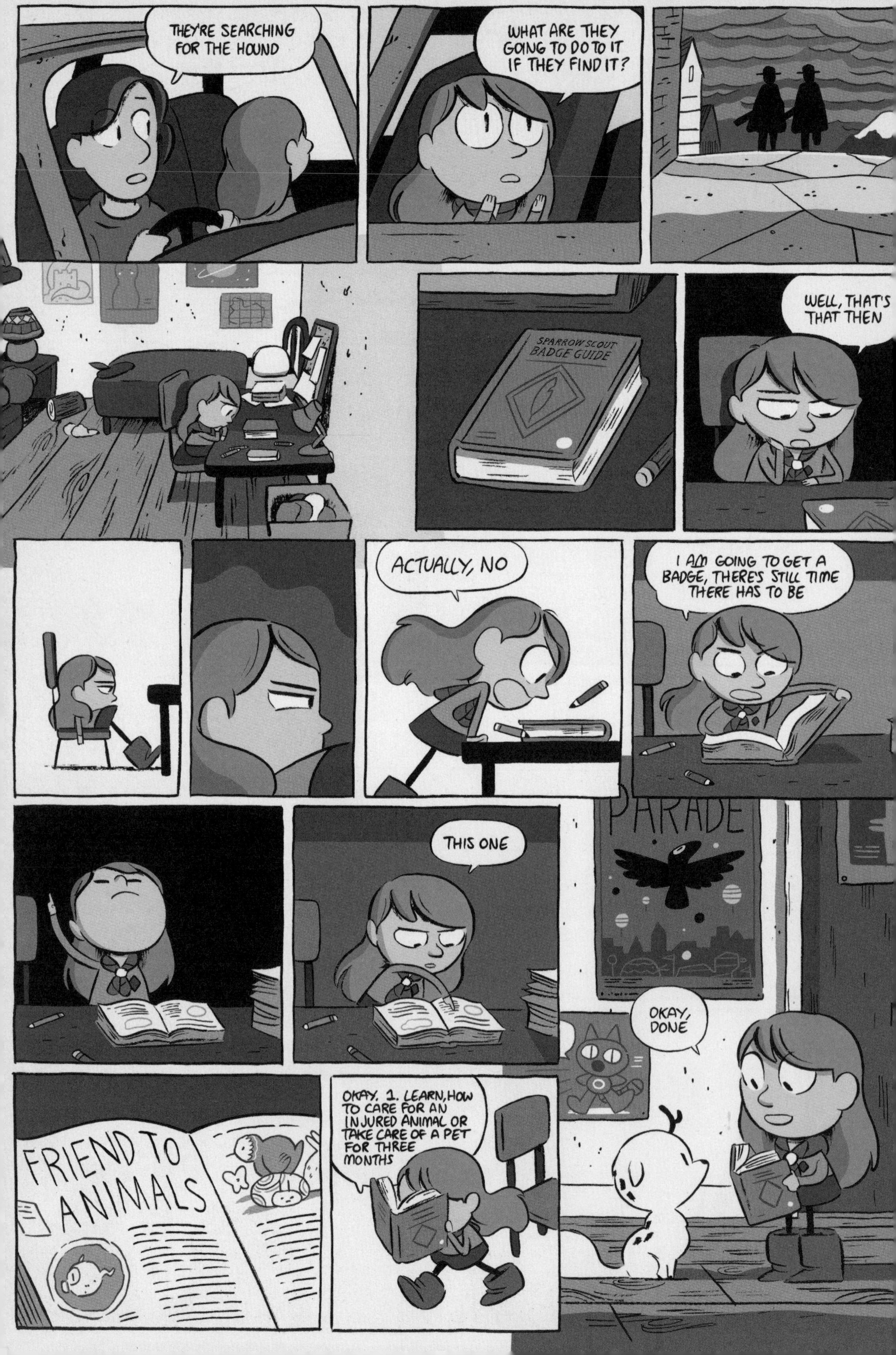
THEY'RE SEARCHING FOR THE HOUND
WHAT ARE THEY GOING TO DO TO IT IF THEY FIND IT?
SPARROW SCOUT BADGE GUIDE
WELL, THAT'S THAT THEN
ACTUALLY, NO
I AM GOING TO GET A BADGE, THERE'S STILL TIME THERE HAS TO BE
THIS ONE
PARADE
OKAY, DONE
FRIEND TO ANIMALS
OKAY. 1. LEARN HOW TO CARE FOR AN INJURED ANIMAL OR TAKE CARE OF A PET FOR THREE MONTHS

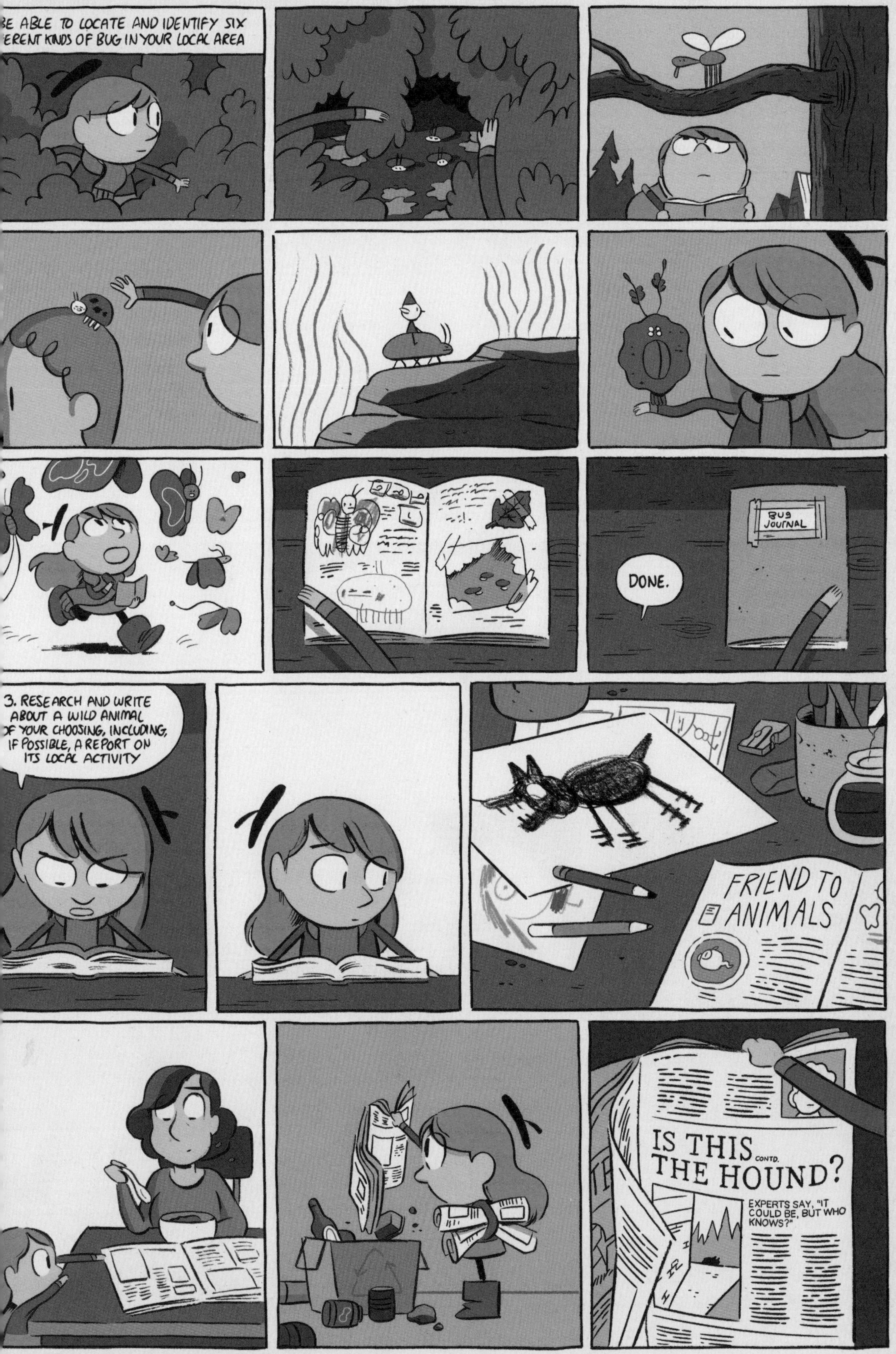

BE ABLE TO LOCATE AND IDENTIFY SIX
ERENT KINDS OF BUG IN YOUR LOCAL AREA
BUG JOURNAL
DONE.
3. RESEARCH AND WRITE ABOUT A WILD ANIMAL OF YOUR CHOOSING, INCLUDING, IF POSSIBLE, A REPORT ON ITS LOCAL ACTIVITY
FRIEND TO ANIMALS
IS THIS CONTD. THE HOUND?
EXPERTS SAY, "IT COULD BE, BUT WHO KNOWS?"

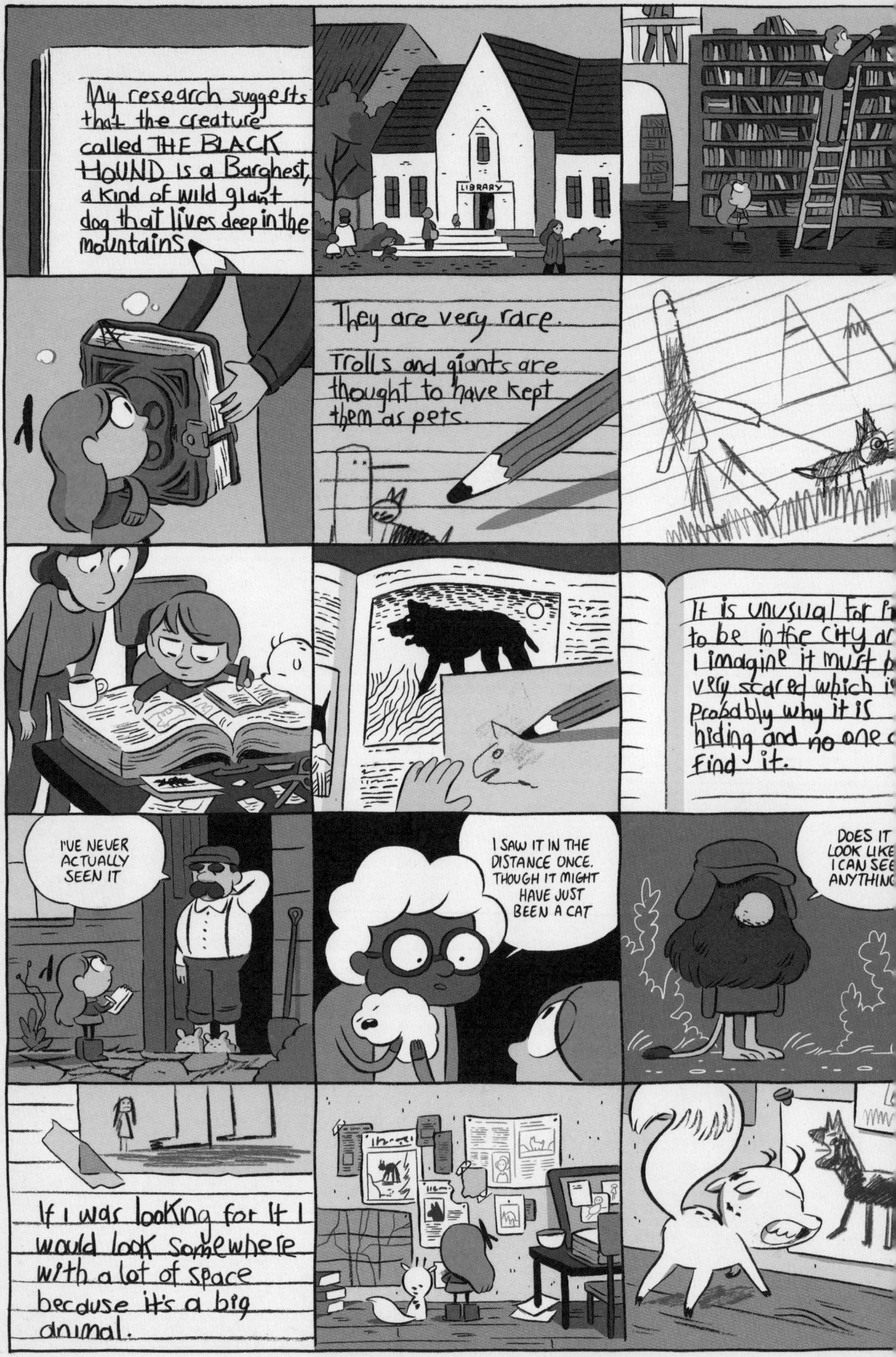
My research suggests that the creature called THE BLACK HOUND is a Barghest, a kind of wild giant dog that lives deep in the mountains
LIBRARY
They are very rare.
Trolls and giants are thought to have kept them as pets.
It is unusual for
to be in the city
I imagine it must
very scared which
Probably why it is
hiding and no one
Find it.
I'VE NEVER ACTUALLY SEEN IT
I SAW IT IN THE DISTANCE ONCE. THOUGH IT MIGHT HAVE JUST BEEN A CAT
DOES IT LOOK LIKE I CAN SEE ANYTHIN
If I was looking for It I would look somewhere with a lot of space because it's a big animal.

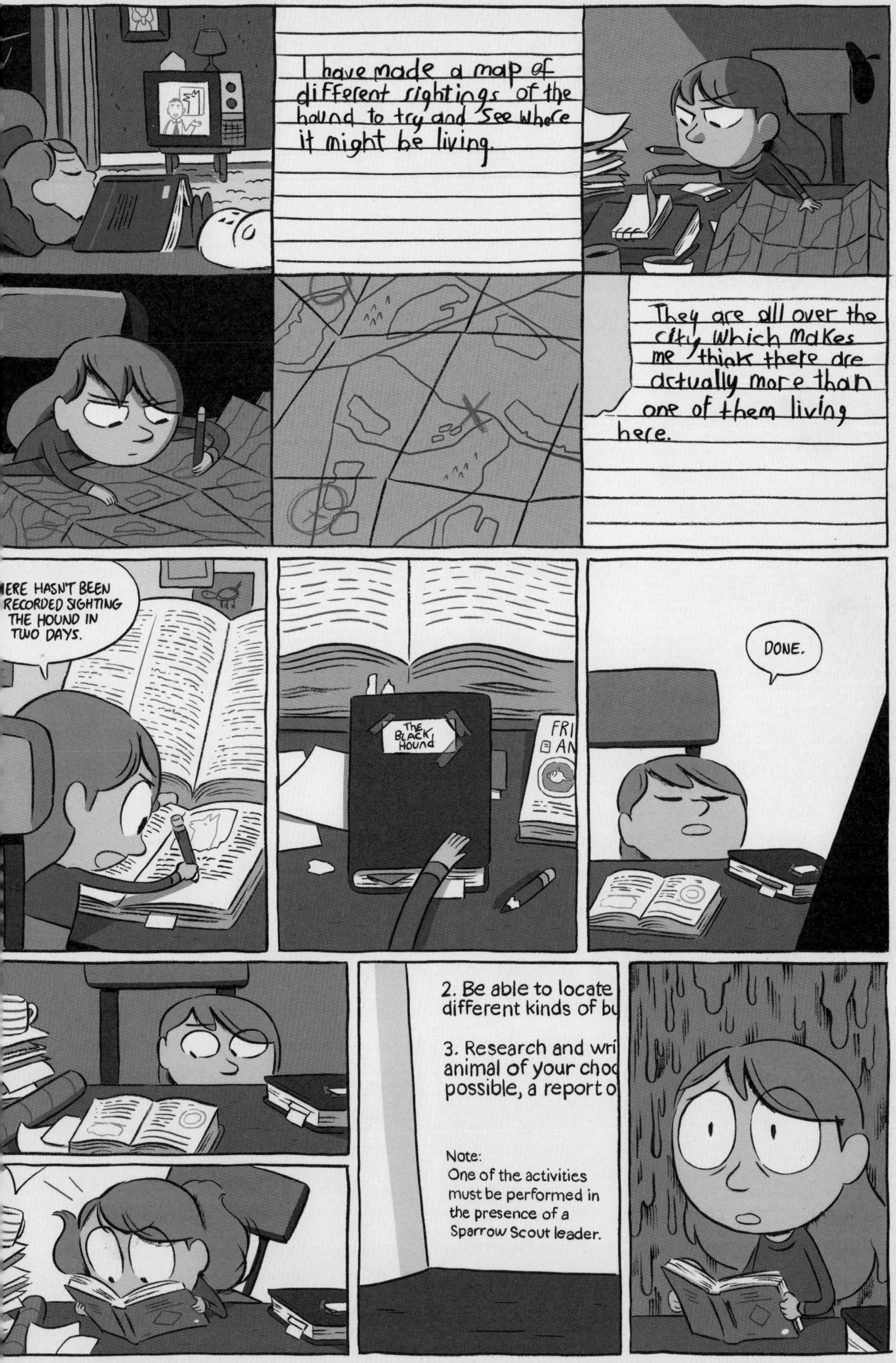

I have made a map of different sightings of the hound to try and see where it might be living.
They are all over the city, which makes me think there are actually more than one of them living here.
HERE HASN'T BEEN RECORDED SIGHTING THE HOUND IN TWO DAYS.
THE BLACK HOUND
DONE.
2. Be able to locate different kinds of bu
3. Research and wri animal of your choo possible, a report o
Note:
One of the activities must be performed in the presence of a Sparrow Scout leader.

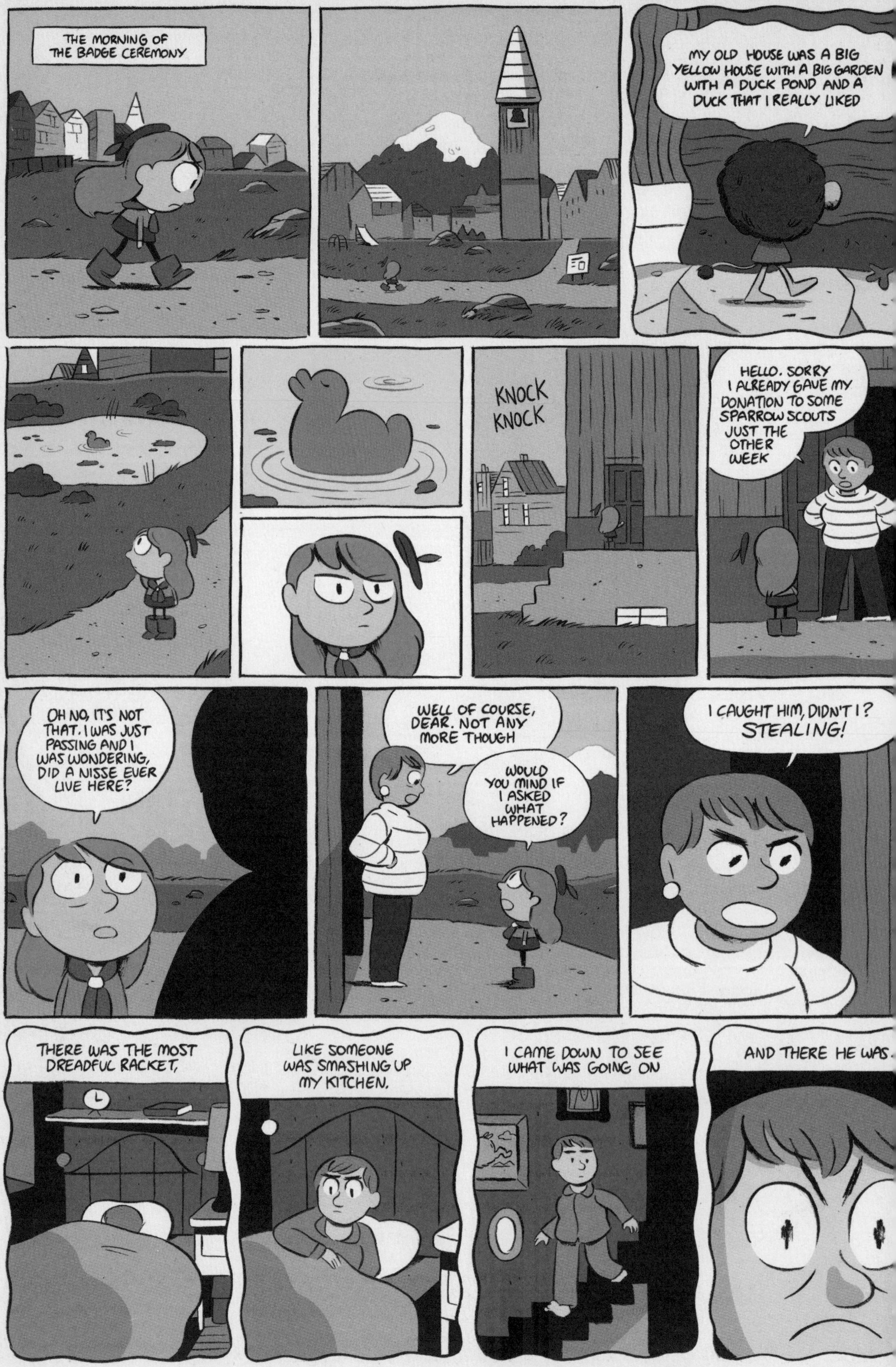
THE MORNING OF THE BADGE CEREMONY
MY OLD HOUSE WAS A BIG YELLOW HOUSE WITH A BIG GARDEN WITH A DUCK POND AND A DUCK THAT I REALLY LIKED
KNOCK KNOCK
HELLO. SORRY I ALREADY GAVE MY DONATION TO SOME SPARROW SCOUTS JUST THE OTHER WEEK
OH NO, IT'S NOT THAT. I WAS JUST PASSING AND I WAS WONDERING, DID A NISSE EVER LIVE HERE?
WELL OF COURSE, DEAR. NOT ANY MORE THOUGH
WOULD YOU MIND IF I ASKED WHAT HAPPENED?
I CAUGHT HIM, DIDN'T I? STEALING!
THERE WAS THE MOST DREADFUL RACKET,
LIKE SOMEONE WAS SMASHING UP MY KITCHEN,
I CAME DOWN TO SEE WHAT WAS GOING ON
AND THERE HE WAS.

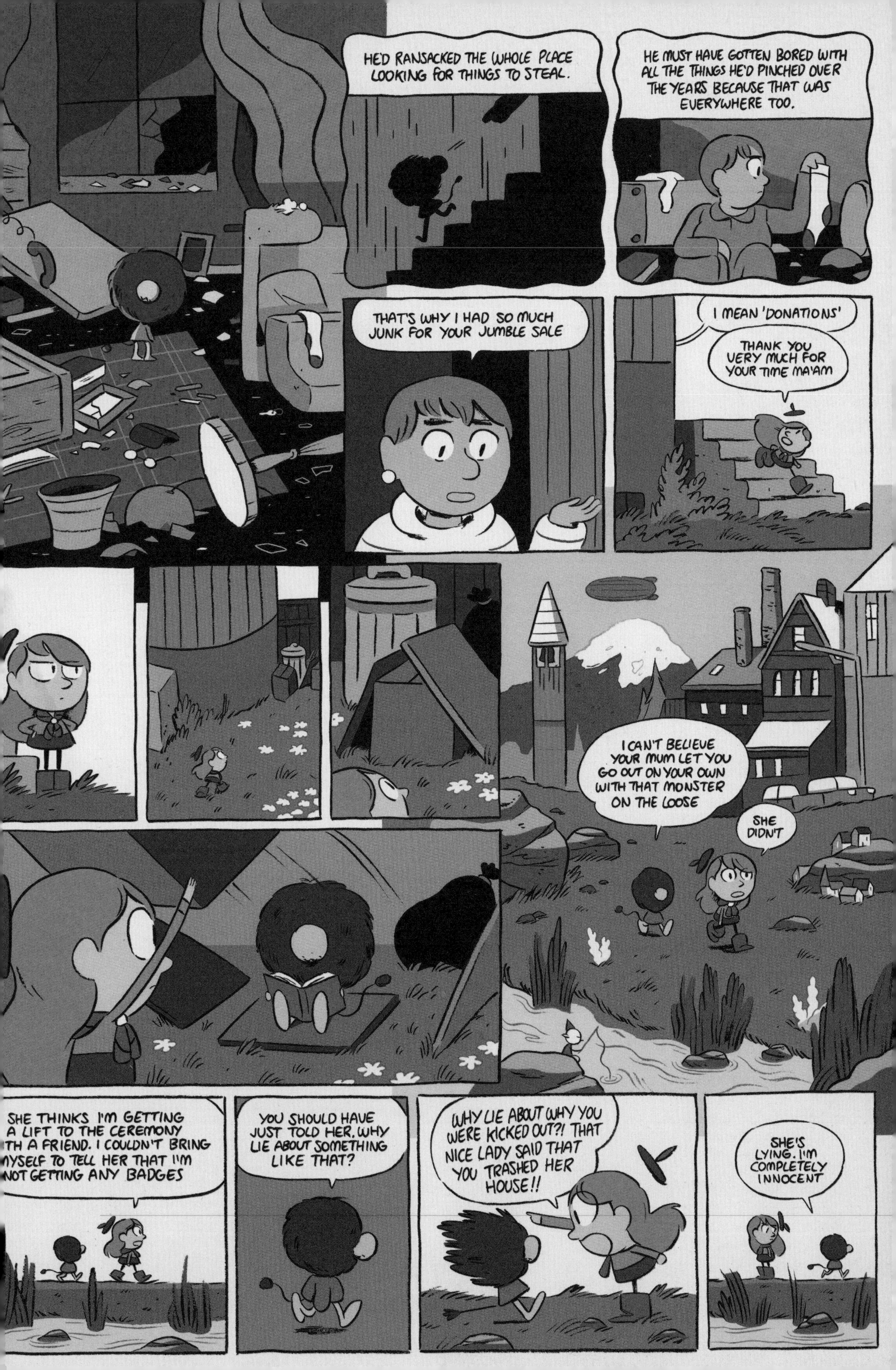
HE'D RANSACKED THE WHOLE PLACE LOOKING FOR THINGS TO STEAL.
HE MUST HAVE GOTTEN BORED WITH ALL THE THINGS HE'D PINCHED OVER THE YEARS BECAUSE THAT WAS EVERYWHERE TOO.
THAT'S WHY I HAD SO MUCH JUNK FOR YOUR JUMBLE SALE
I MEAN 'DONATIONS'
THANK YOU VERY MUCH FOR YOUR TIME MA'AM
I CAN'T BELIEVE YOUR MUM LET YOU GO OUT ON YOUR OWN WITH THAT MONSTER ON THE LOOSE
SHE DIDN'T
SHE THINKS I'M GETTING A LIFT TO THE CEREMONY ITH A FRIEND. I COULDN'T BRING MYSELF TO TELL HER THAT I'M NOT GETTING ANY BADGES
YOU SHOULD HAVE JUST TOLD HER. WHY LIE ABOUT SOMETHING LIKE THAT?
WHY LIE ABOUT WHY YOU WERE KICKED OUT?! THAT NICE LADY SAID THAT YOU TRASHED HER HOUSE!!
SHE'S LYING. I'M COMPLETELY INNOCENT

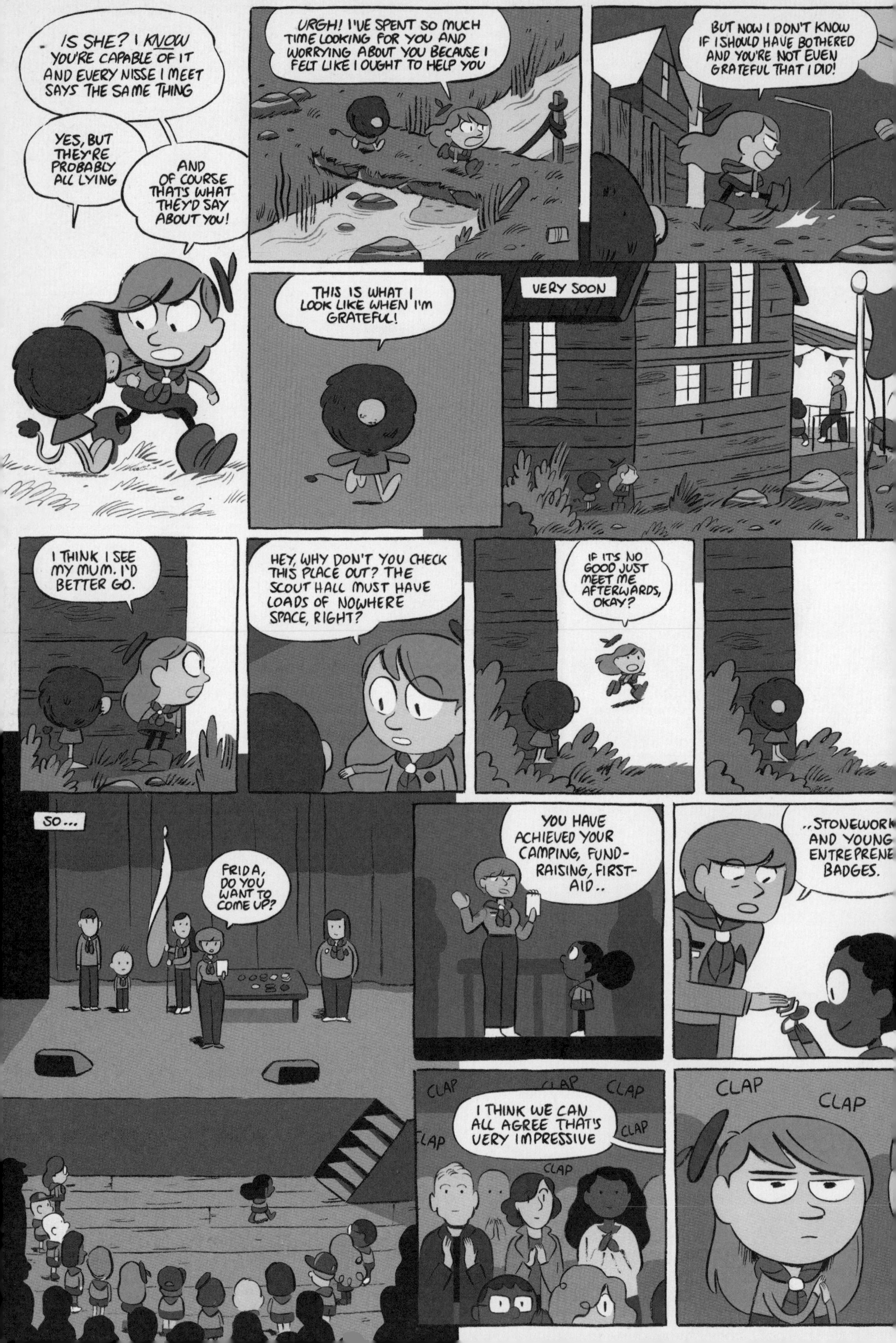

IS SHE? I KNOW YOU'RE CAPABLE OF IT AND EVERY NISSE I MEET SAYS THE SAME THING
YES, BUT THEY'RE PROBABLY ALL LYING
AND OF COURSE THAT'S WHAT THEY'D SAY ABOUT YOU!
URGH! I'VE SPENT SO MUCH TIME LOOKING FOR YOU AND WORRYING ABOUT YOU BECAUSE I FELT LIKE I OUGHT TO HELP YOU
BUT NOW I DON'T KNOW IF I SHOULD HAVE BOTHERED AND YOU'RE NOT EVEN GRATEFUL THAT I DID!
THIS IS WHAT I LOOK LIKE WHEN I'M GRATEFUL!
VERY SOON
I THINK I SEE MY MUM. I'D BETTER GO.
HEY, WHY DON'T YOU CHECK THIS PLACE OUT? THE SCOUT HALL MUST HAVE LOADS OF NOWHERE SPACE, RIGHT?
IF IT'S NO GOOD JUST MEET ME AFTERWARDS, OKAY?
SO...
FRIDA, DO YOU WANT TO COME UP?
YOU HAVE ACHIEVED YOUR CAMPING, FUND-RAISING, FIRST-AID..
..STONEWORK AND YOUNG ENTREPRENE BADGES.
CLAP
CLAP
CLAP
I THINK WE CAN ALL AGREE THAT'S VERY IMPRESSIVE
CLAP
CLAP
CLAP
CLAP
CLAP

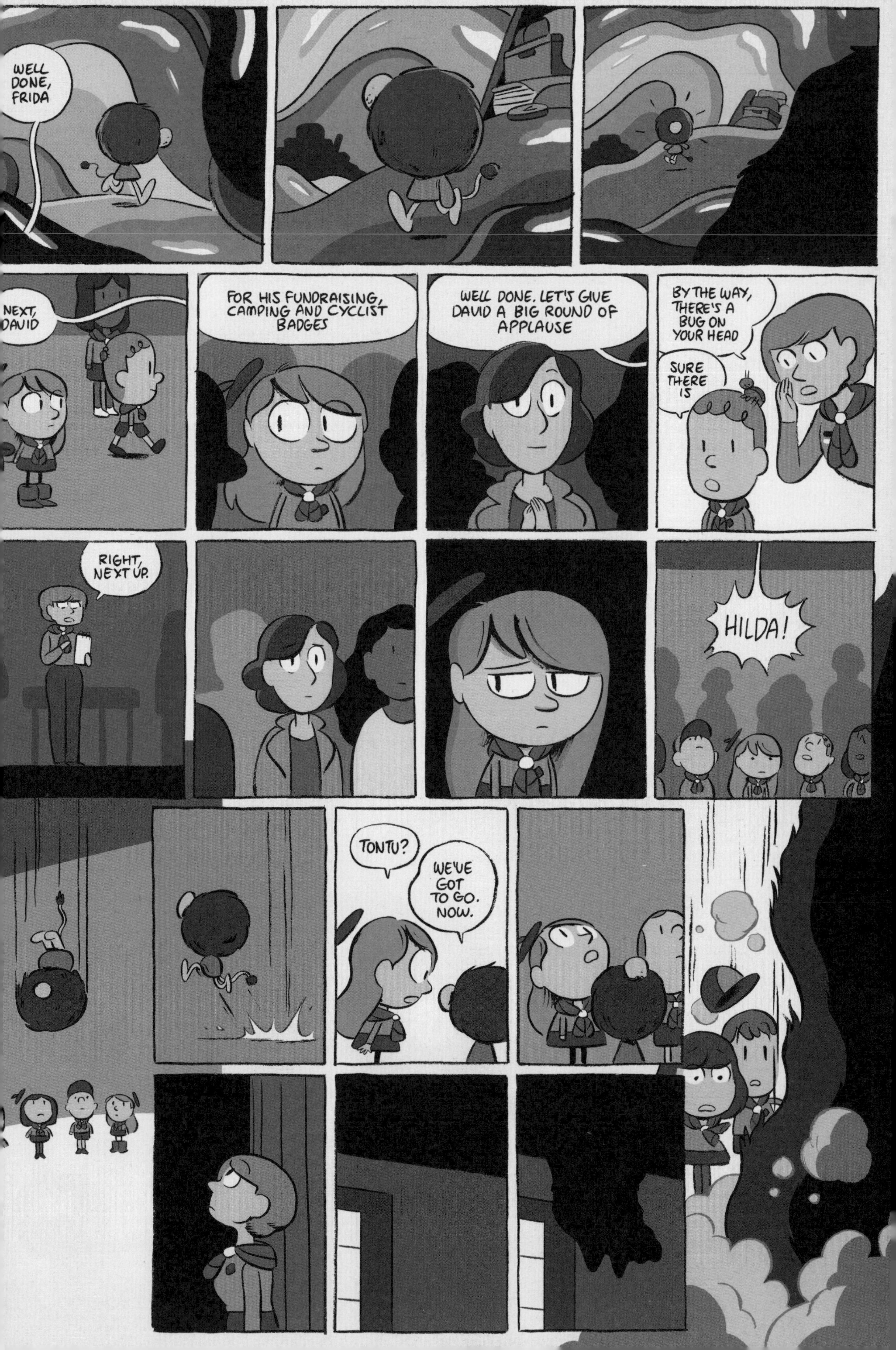

WELL DONE, FRIDA
NEXT, DAVID
FOR HIS FUNDRAISING, CAMPING AND CYCLIST BADGES
WELL DONE. LET'S GIVE DAVID A BIG ROUND OF APPLAUSE
BY THE WAY, THERE'S A BUG ON YOUR HEAD
SURE THERE IS
RIGHT, NEXT UP.
HILDA!
TONTU?
WE'VE GOT TO GO. NOW.

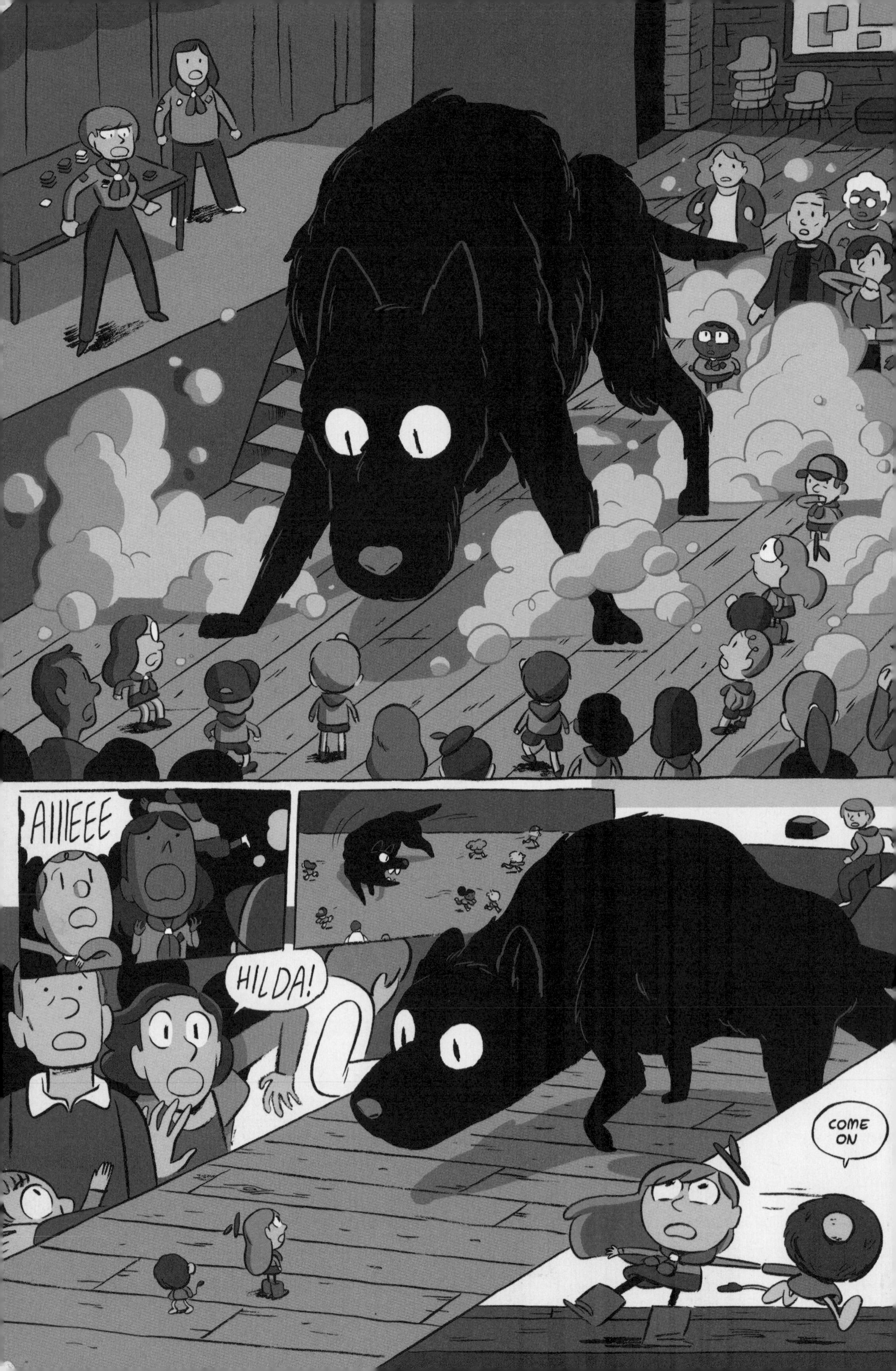
AIIIEEE
HILDA!
COME ON

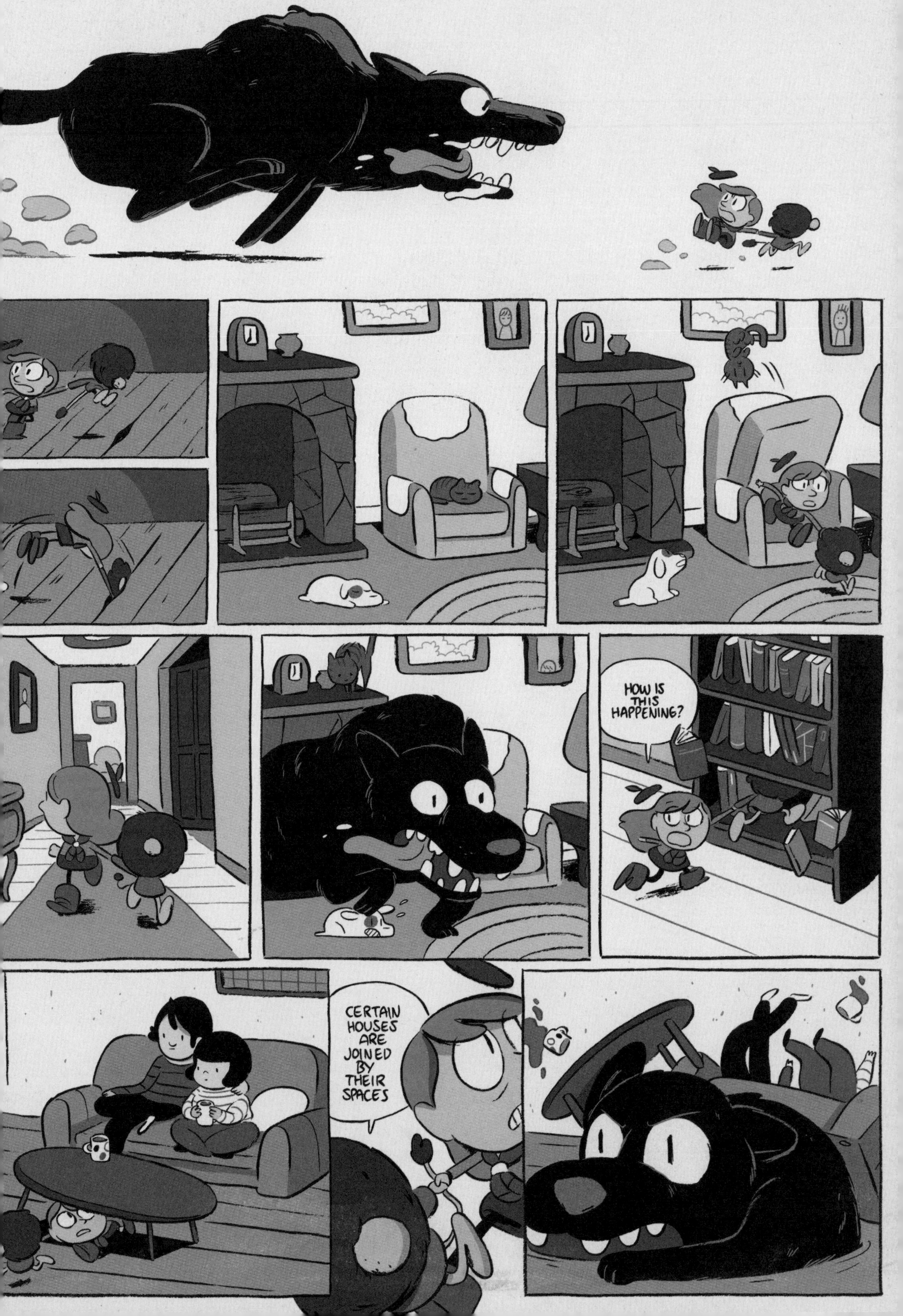
HOW IS THIS HAPPENING?
CERTAIN HOUSES ARE JOINED BY THEIR SPACES

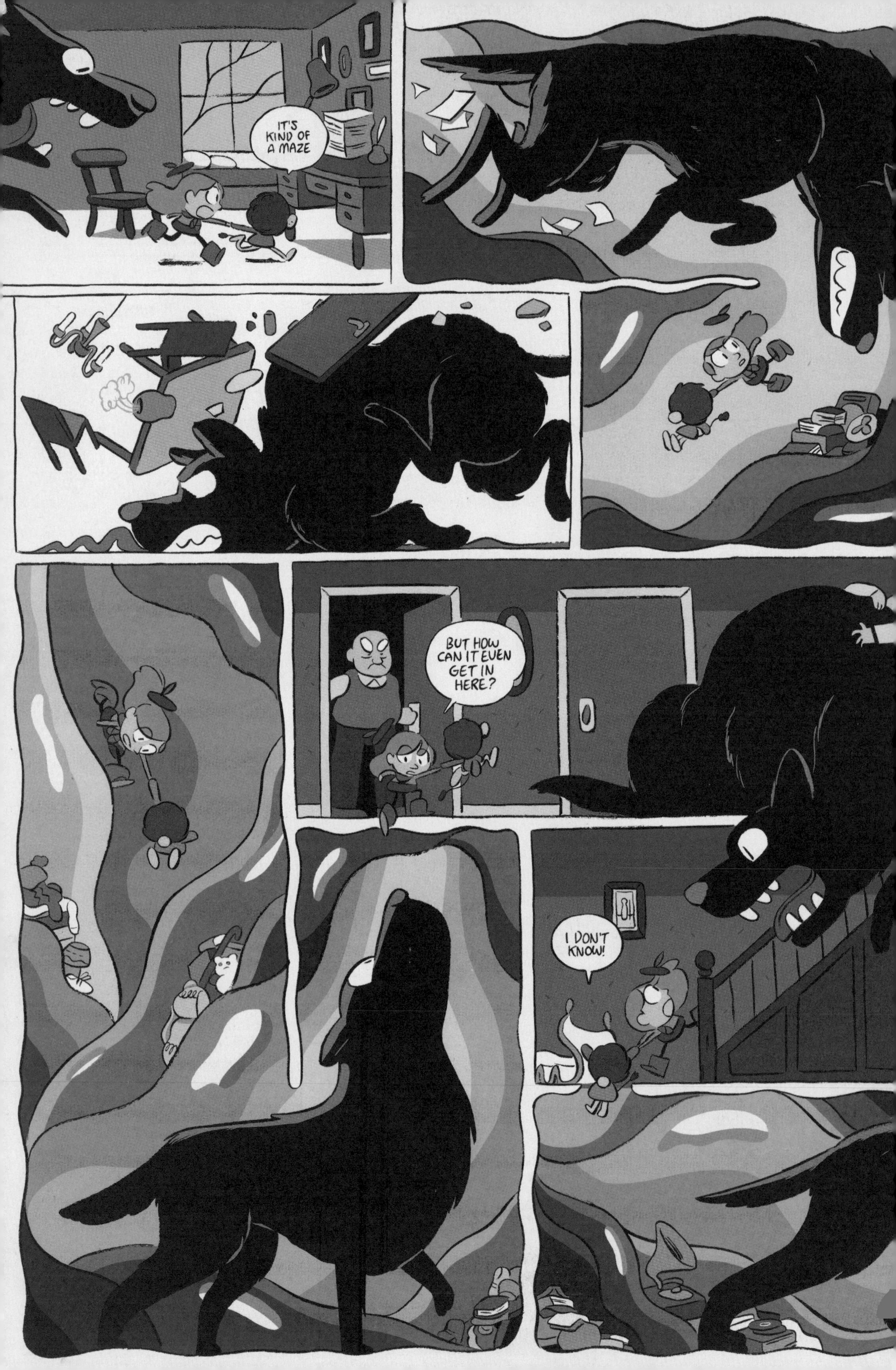
IT'S KIND OF A MAZE
BUT HOW CAN IT EVEN GET IN HERE?
I DON'T KNOW!

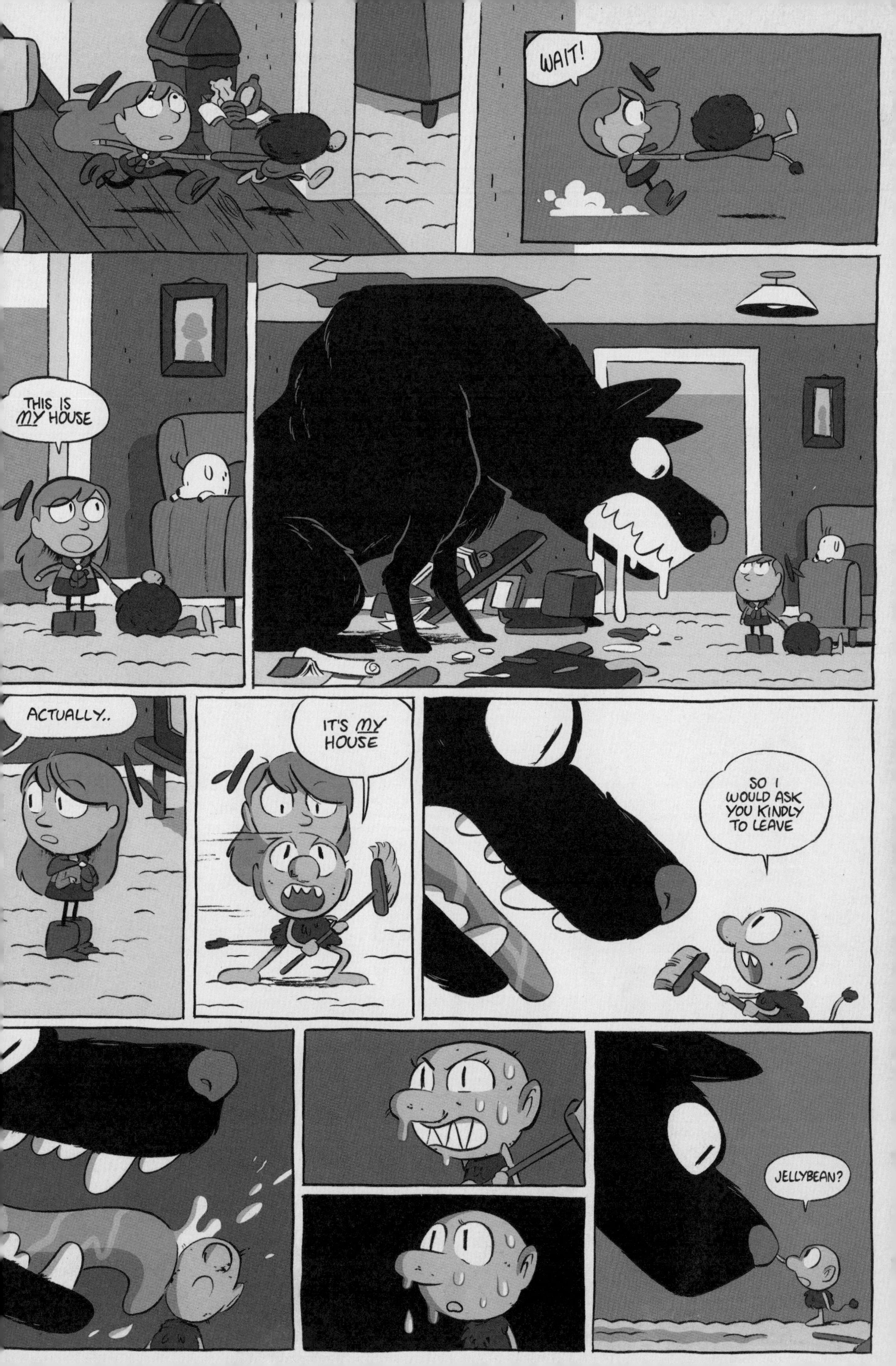
WAIT!
THIS IS MY HOUSE
ACTUALLY..
IT'S MY HOUSE
SO I WOULD ASK YOU KINDLY TO LEAVE
JELLYBEAN?

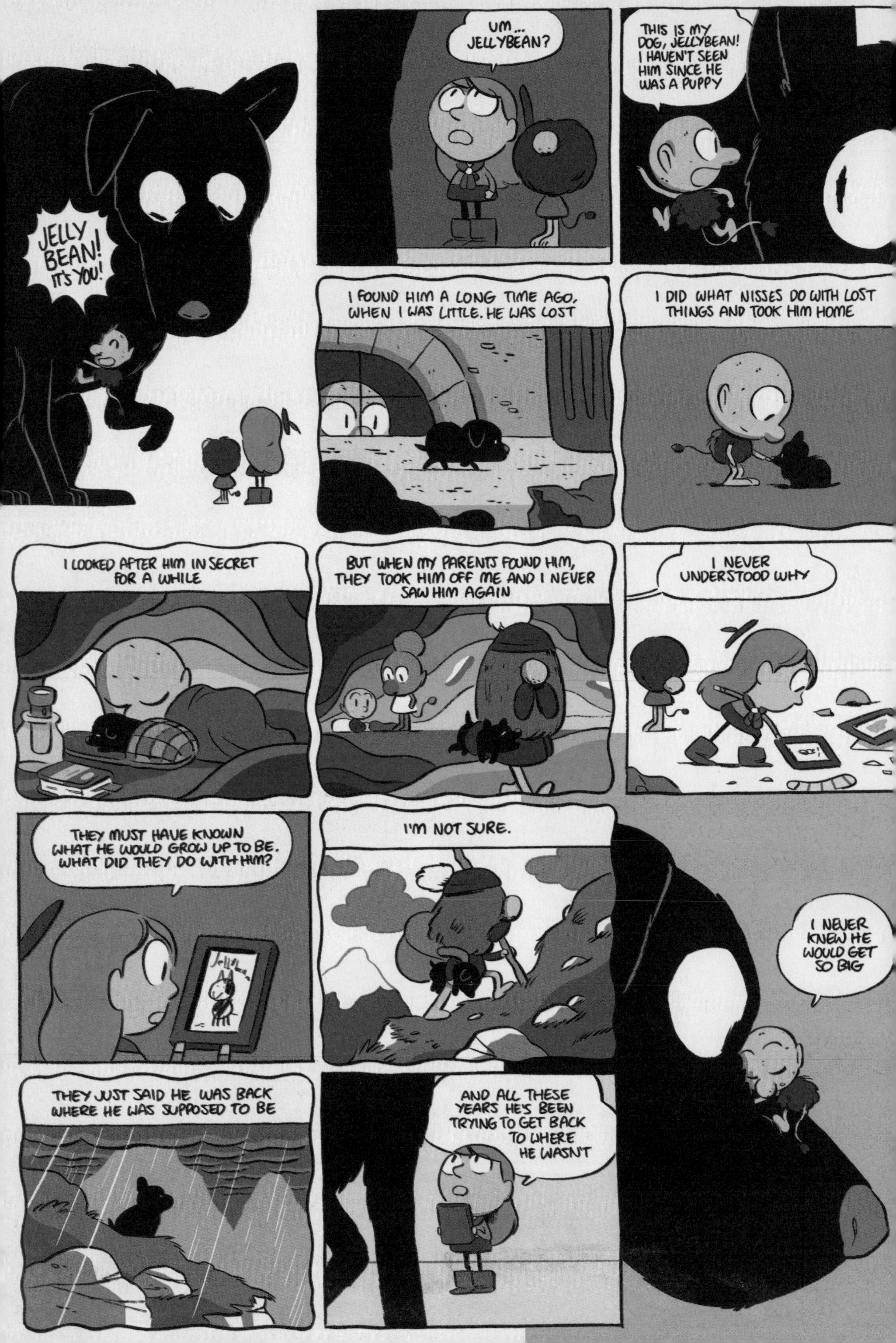
JELLY BEAN! IT'S YOU!
UM... JELLYBEAN?
THIS IS MY DOG, JELLYBEAN! I HAVEN'T SEEN HIM SINCE HE WAS A PUPPY
I FOUND HIM A LONG TIME AGO, WHEN I WAS LITTLE. HE WAS LOST
I DID WHAT NISSES DO WITH LOST THINGS AND TOOK HIM HOME
I LOOKED AFTER HIM IN SECRET FOR A WHILE
BUT WHEN MY PARENTS FOUND HIM, THEY TOOK HIM OFF ME AND I NEVER SAW HIM AGAIN
I NEVER UNDERSTOOD WHY
THEY MUST HAVE KNOWN WHAT HE WOULD GROW UP TO BE. WHAT DID THEY DO WITH HIM?
I'M NOT SURE.
I NEVER KNEW HE WOULD GET SO BIG
THEY JUST SAID HE WAS BACK WHERE HE WAS SUPPOSED TO BE
AND ALL THESE YEARS HE'S BEEN TRYING TO GET BACK TO WHERE HE WASN'T

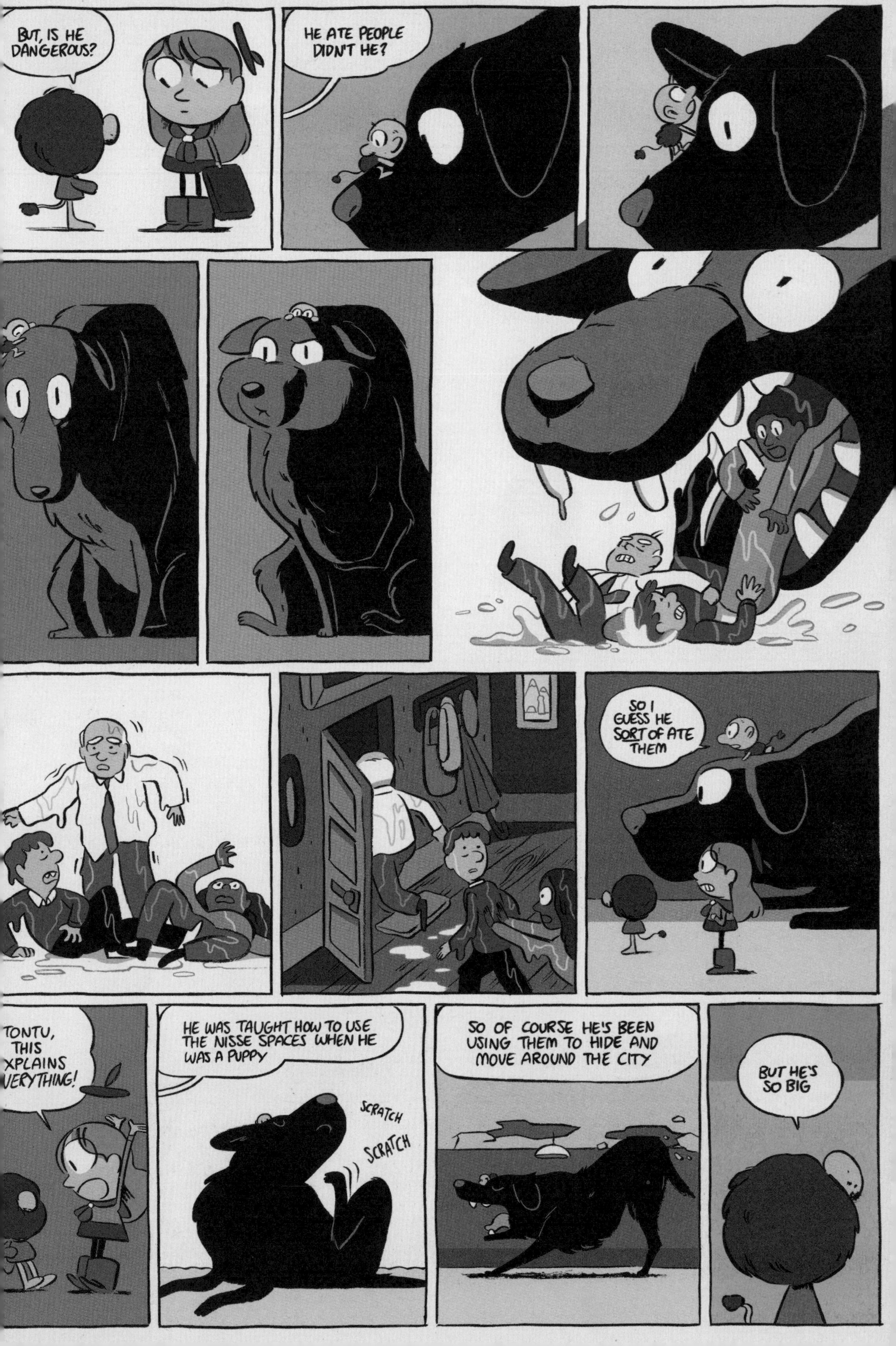
BUT, IS HE DANGEROUS?
HE ATE PEOPLE DIDN'T HE?
SO I GUESS HE SORT OF ATE THEM
TONTU, THIS XPLAINS VERYTHING!
HE WAS TAUGHT HOW TO USE THE NISSE SPACES WHEN HE WAS A PUPPY
SCRATCH
SCRATCH
SO OF COURSE HE'S BEEN USING THEM TO HIDE AND MOVE AROUND THE CITY
BUT HE'S SO BIG

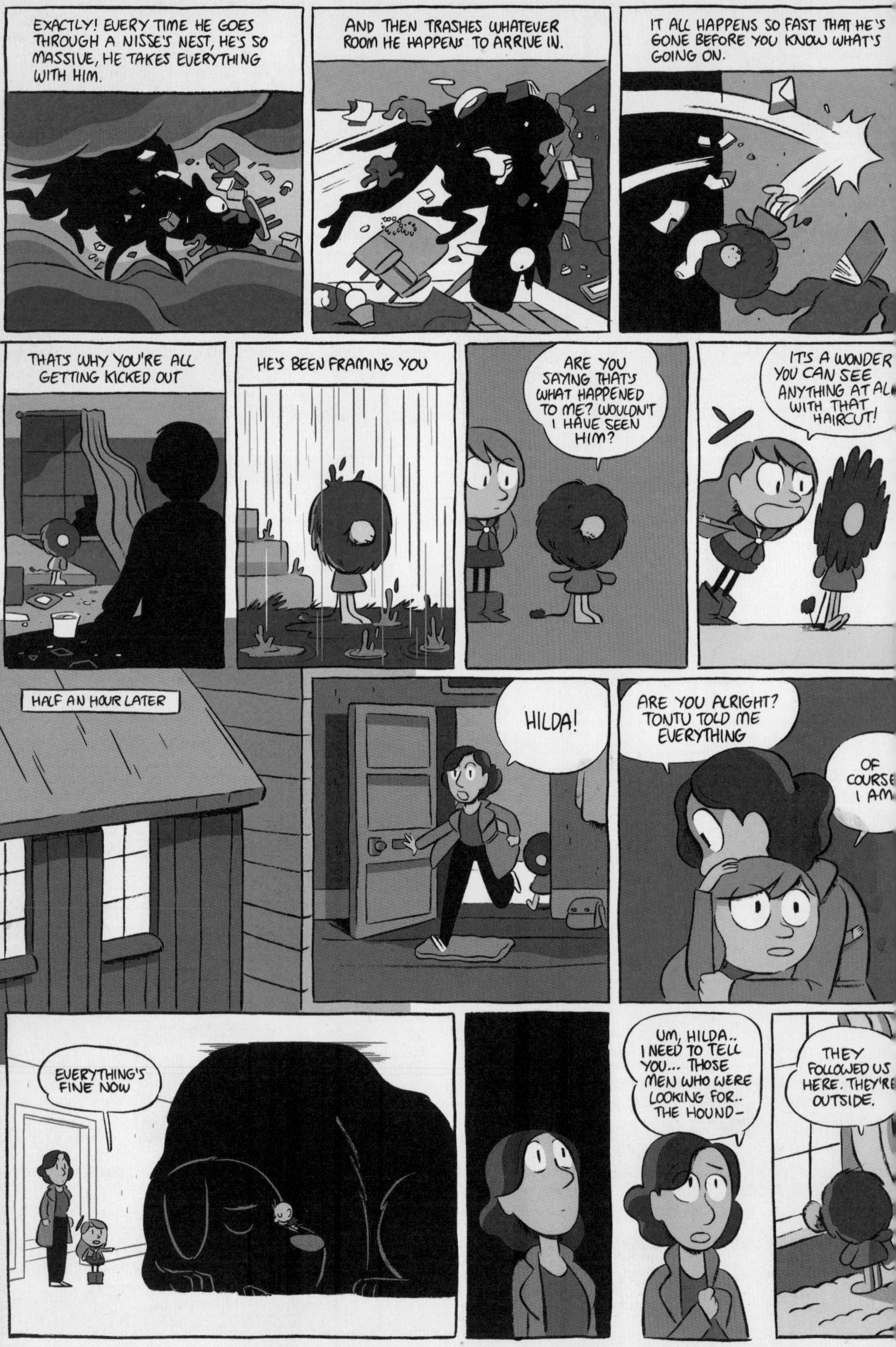

EXACTLY! EVERY TIME HE GOES THROUGH A NISSE'S NEST, HE'S SO MASSIVE, HE TAKES EVERYTHING WITH HIM.
AND THEN TRASHES WHATEVER ROOM HE HAPPENS TO ARRIVE IN.
IT ALL HAPPENS SO FAST THAT HE'S GONE BEFORE YOU KNOW WHAT'S GOING ON.
THAT'S WHY YOU'RE ALL GETTING KICKED OUT
HE'S BEEN FRAMING YOU
ARE YOU SAYING THAT'S WHAT HAPPENED TO ME? WOULDN'T I HAVE SEEN HIM?
IT'S A WONDER YOU CAN SEE ANYTHING AT AL WITH THAT HAIRCUT!
HALF AN HOUR LATER
HILDA!
ARE YOU ALRIGHT? TONTU TOLD ME EVERYTHING
OF COURSE I AM
EVERYTHING'S FINE NOW
UM, HILDA.. I NEED TO TELL YOU... THOSE MEN WHO WERE LOOKING FOR.. THE HOUND-
THEY FOLLOWED US HERE. THEY'RE OUTSIDE.

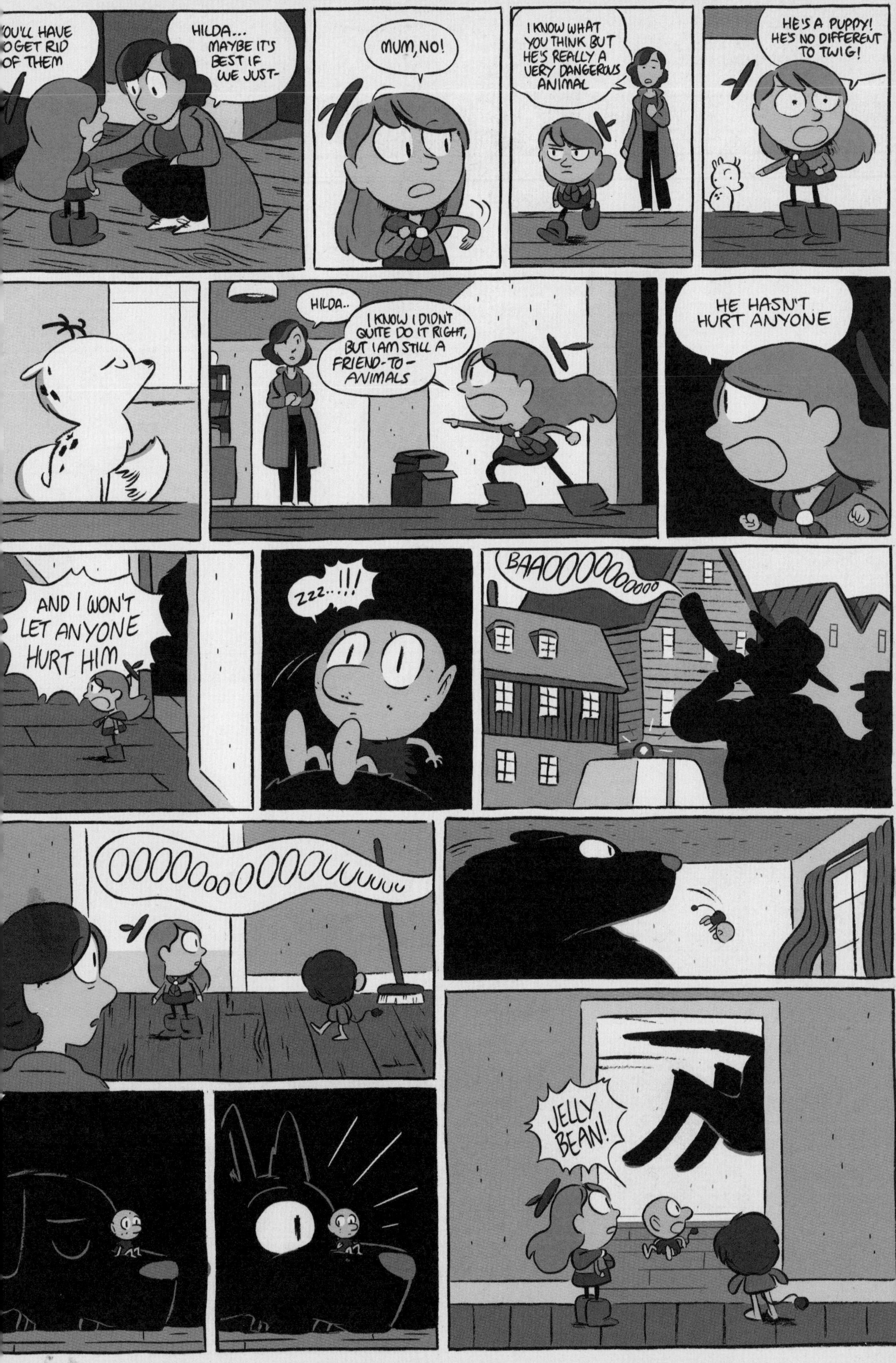
YOU'LL HAVE TO GET RID OF THEM
HILDA... MAYBE IT'S BEST IF WE JUST-
MUM, NO!
I KNOW WHAT YOU THINK BUT HE'S REALLY A VERY DANGEROUS ANIMAL
HE'S A PUPPY! HE'S NO DIFFERENT TO TWIG!
HILDA..
I KNOW I DIDN'T QUITE DO IT RIGHT, BUT I AM STILL A FRIEND-TO-ANIMALS
HE HASN'T HURT ANYONE
AND I WON'T LET ANYONE HURT HIM
ZZZ..!!!
BAAOOOOOOOoooo
OOOOOooOOOOUUUUUU
JELLY BEAN!

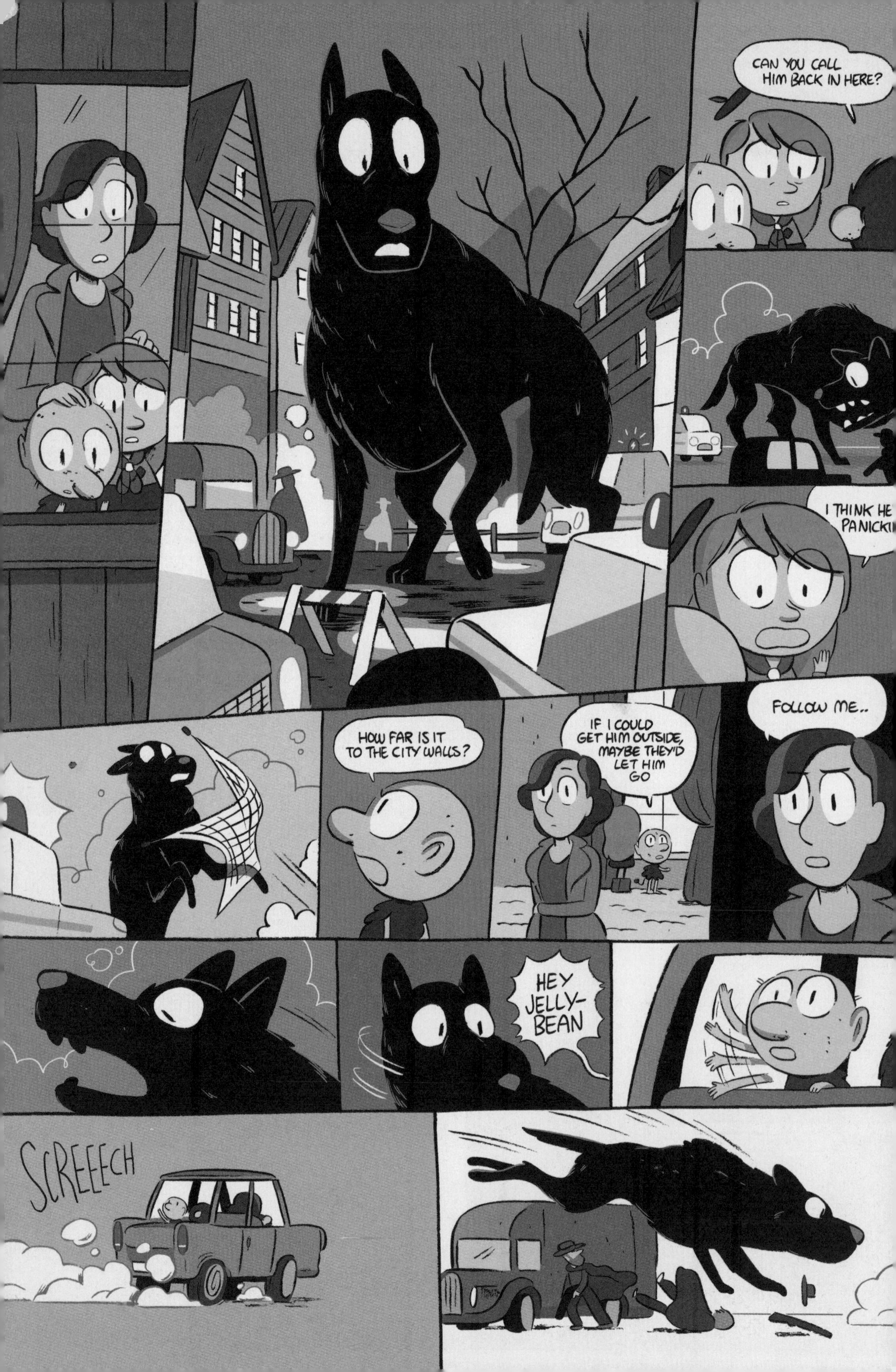
CAN YOU CALL HIM BACK IN HERE?
I THINK HE'
PANICKI
HOW FAR IS IT TO THE CITY WALLS?
IF I COULD GET HIM OUTSIDE, MAYBE THEY'D LET HIM GO
FOLLOW ME..
HEY JELLY-BEAN
SCREEECH

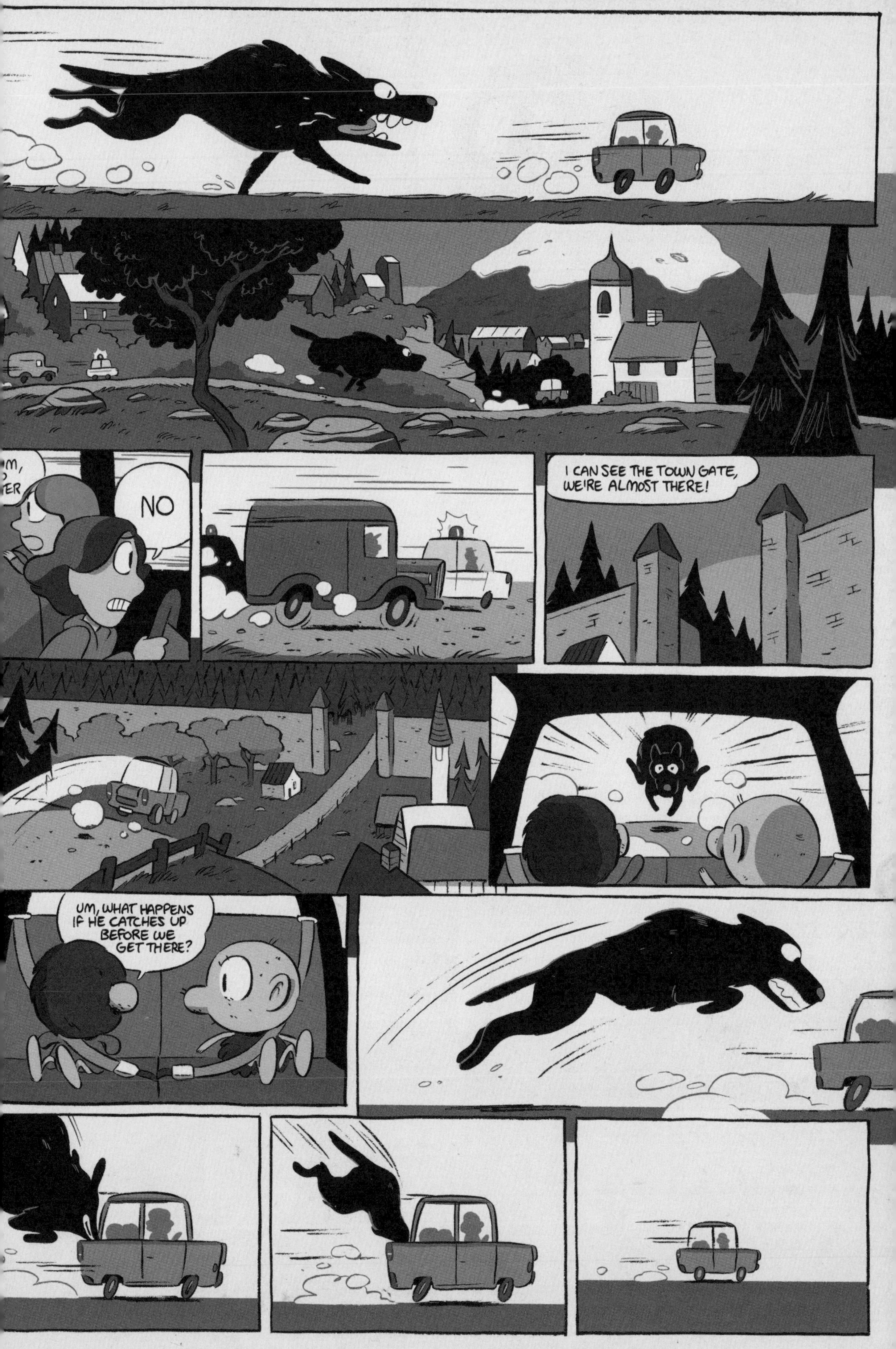
NO
I CAN SEE THE TOWN GATE, WE'RE ALMOST THERE!
UM, WHAT HAPPENS IF HE CATCHES UP BEFORE WE GET THERE?

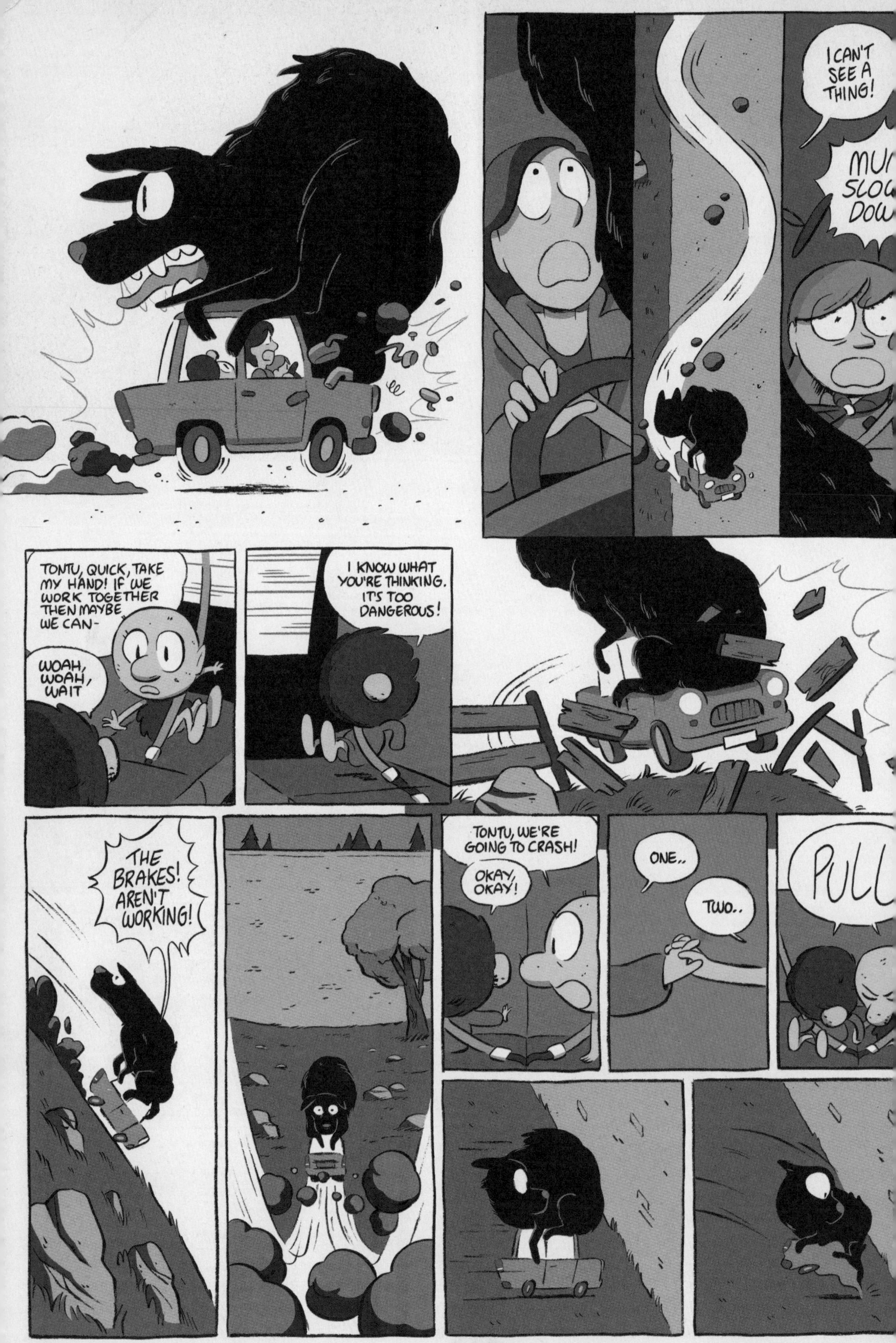
I CAN'T SEE A THING!
MUM SLOW DOW
TONTU, QUICK, TAKE MY HAND! IF WE WORK TOGETHER THEN MAYBE WE CAN-
WOAH, WOAH, WAIT
I KNOW WHAT YOU'RE THINKING. IT'S TOO DANGEROUS!
THE BRAKES! AREN'T WORKING!
TONTU, WE'RE GOING TO CRASH!
OKAY, OKAY!
ONE..
TWO..
PULL

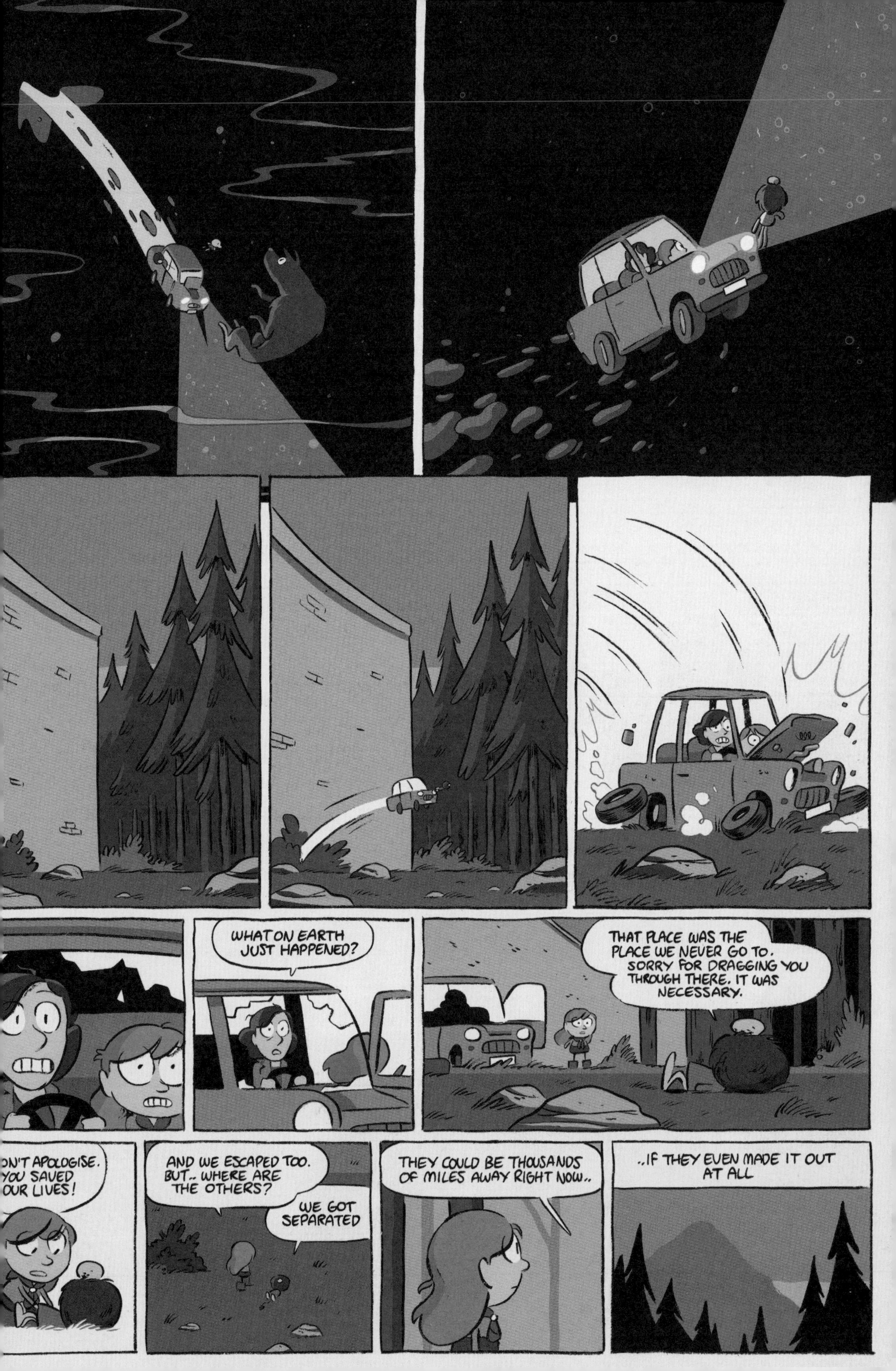
WHAT ON EARTH JUST HAPPENED?
THAT PLACE WAS THE PLACE WE NEVER GO TO. SORRY FOR DRAGGING YOU THROUGH THERE. IT WAS NECESSARY.
ON'T APOLOGISE. YOU SAVED OUR LIVES!
AND WE ESCAPED TOO. BUT.. WHERE ARE THE OTHERS?
WE GOT SEPARATED
THEY COULD BE THOUSANDS OF MILES AWAY RIGHT NOW..
..IF THEY EVEN MADE IT OUT AT ALL

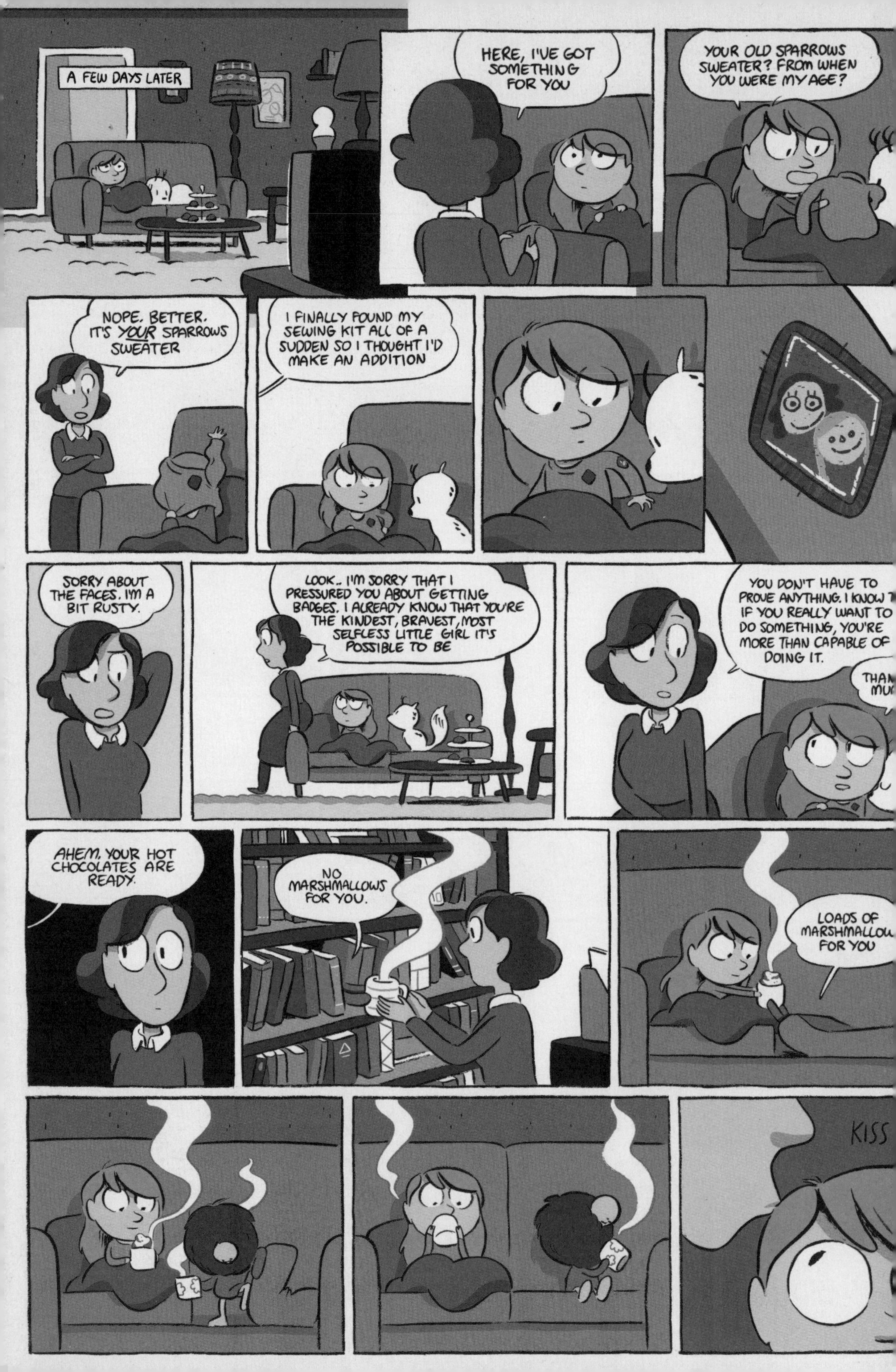
A FEW DAYS LATER
HERE, I'VE GOT SOMETHING FOR YOU
YOUR OLD SPARROWS SWEATER? FROM WHEN YOU WERE MY AGE?
NOPE. BETTER. IT'S YOUR SPARROWS SWEATER
I FINALLY FOUND MY SEWING KIT ALL OF A SUDDEN SO I THOUGHT I'D MAKE AN ADDITION
SORRY ABOUT THE FACES. I'M A BIT RUSTY.
LOOK.. I'M SORRY THAT I PRESSURED YOU ABOUT GETTING BADGES. I ALREADY KNOW THAT YOU'RE THE KINDEST, BRAVEST, MOST SELFLESS LITTLE GIRL IT'S POSSIBLE TO BE
YOU DON'T HAVE TO PROVE ANYTHING. I KNOW IF YOU REALLY WANT TO DO SOMETHING, YOU'RE MORE THAN CAPABLE OF DOING IT.
AHEM. YOUR HOT CHOCOLATES ARE READY.
NO MARSHMALLOWS FOR YOU.
LOADS OF MARSHMALLOWS FOR YOU
KISS

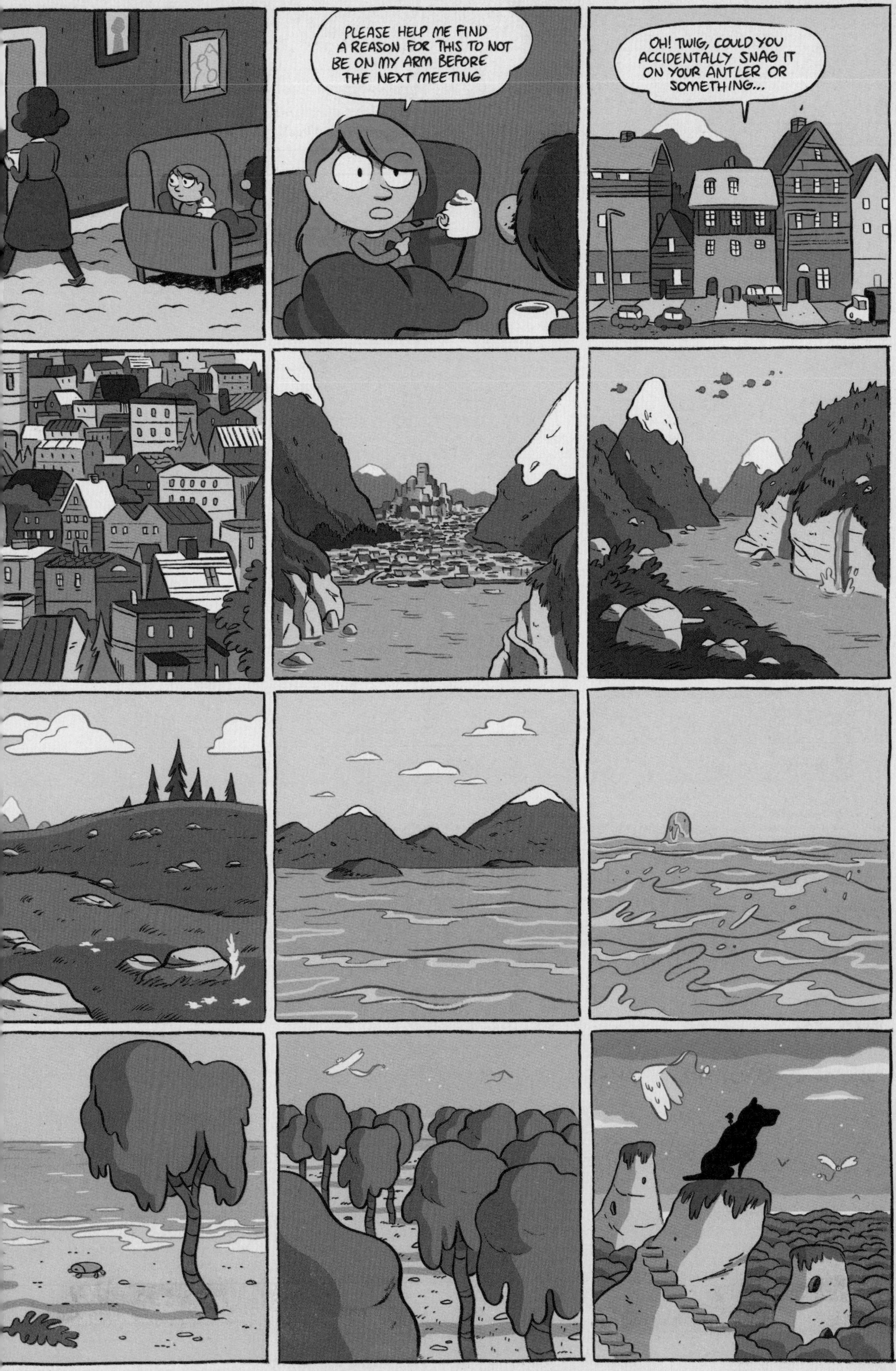
PLEASE HELP ME FIND A REASON FOR THIS TO NOT BE ON MY ARM BEFORE THE NEXT MEETING
OH! TWIG, COULD YOU ACCIDENTALLY SNAG IT ON YOUR ANTLER OR SOMETHING...

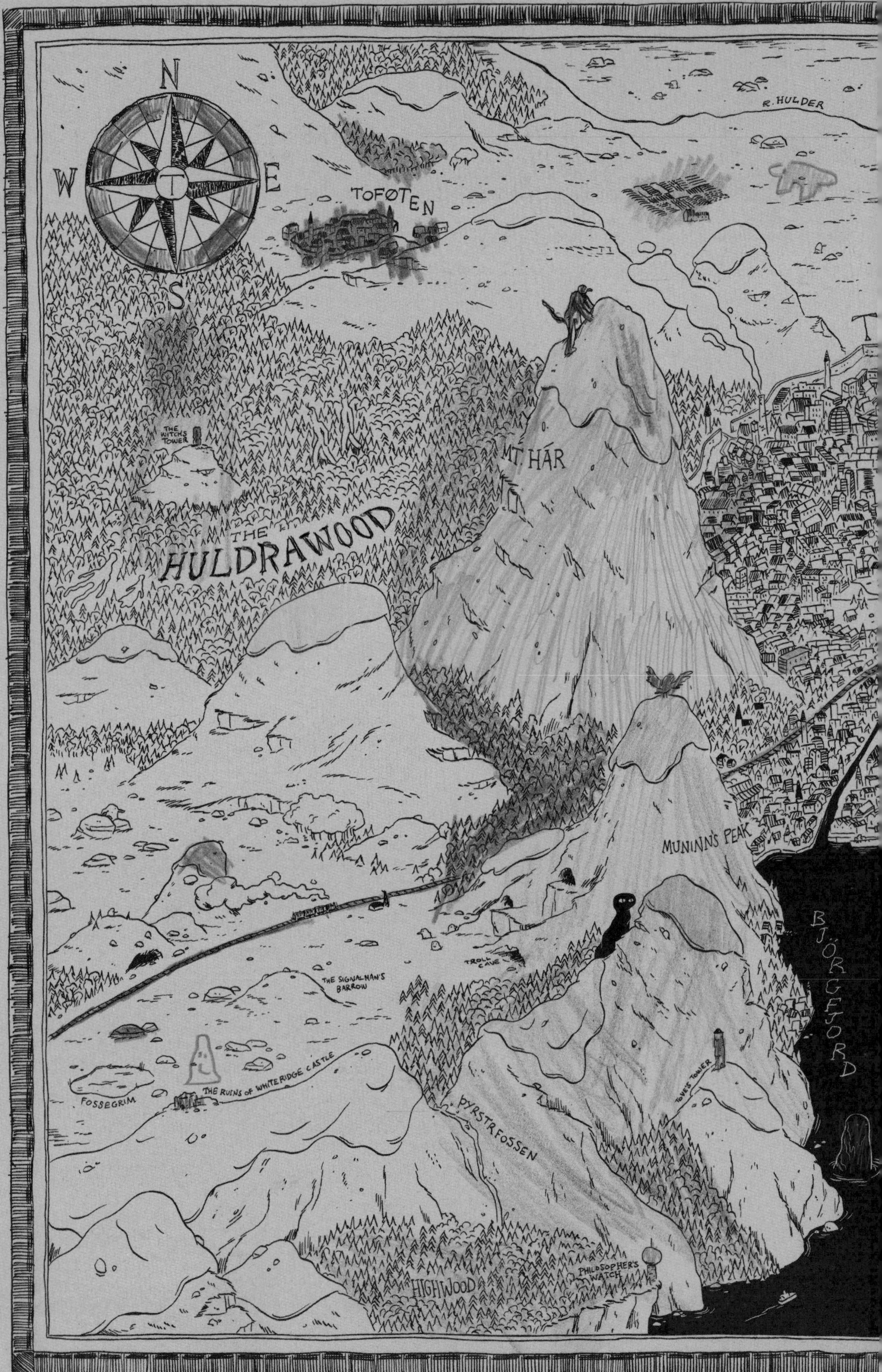

N
W
E
S
T
TOFØTEN
R. HULDER
THE WITCH'S TOWER
MT. HÁR
THE HULDRAWOOD
MUNINN'S PEAK
BJÖRGFJORD
TROLL CAVE
THE SIGNALMAN'S BARROW
THE RUINS OF WHITERIDGE CASTLE
FOSSEGRIM
ÞYRSTRFOSSEN
TOVE'S TOWER
PHILOSOPHER'S WATCH
HIGHWOOD

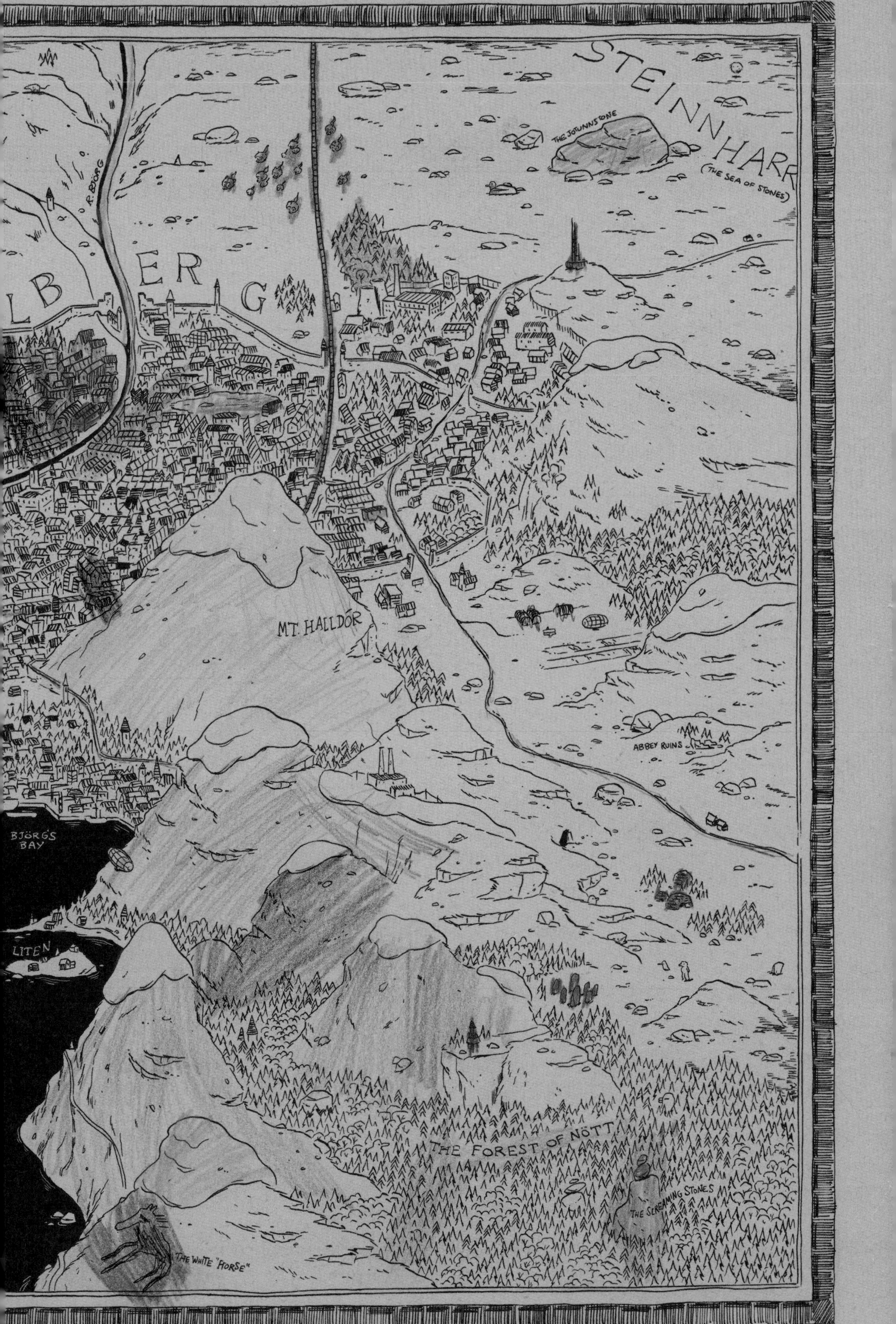

STEINNHARR
(THE SEA OF STONES)
THE JOTUNNSTONE
R. BJÖRG
LBERG
MT. HALLDÓR
ABBEY RUINS
BJÖRG'S BAY
LITEN
THE FOREST OF NÖTT
THE SCREAMING STONES
THE WHITE "HORSE"

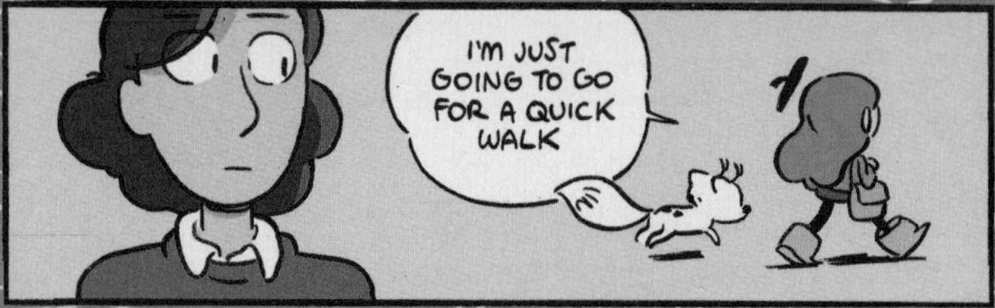
I'M JUST GOING TO GO FOR A QUICK WALK

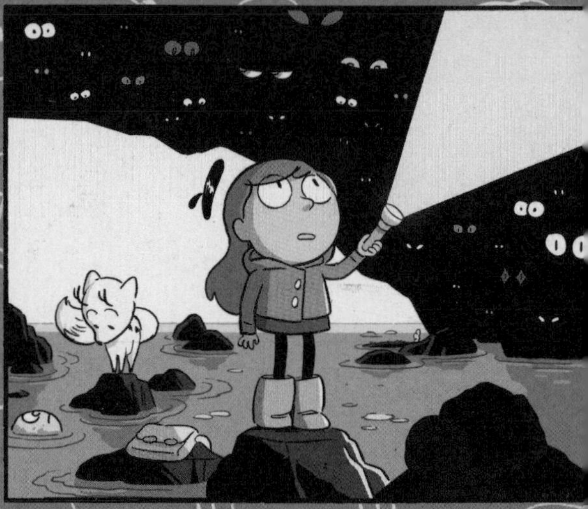

HILDA IS HARDLY AT HOME ANY MORE, SEEKING DAYS FILLED WITH ADVENTURE AND EXCITEMENT... AND HER MUM IS STARTING TO WORRY.

IN HILDA'S NEXT ADVENTURE

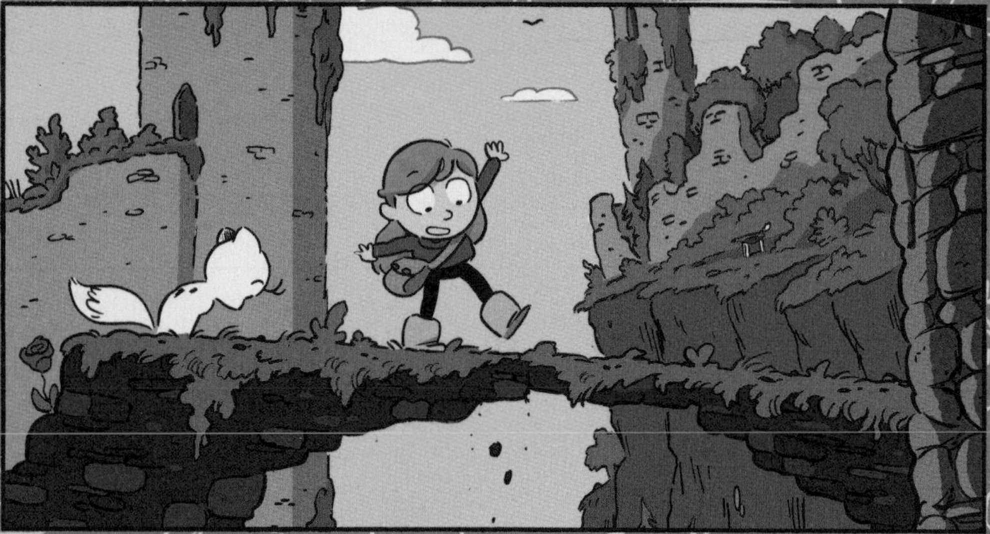

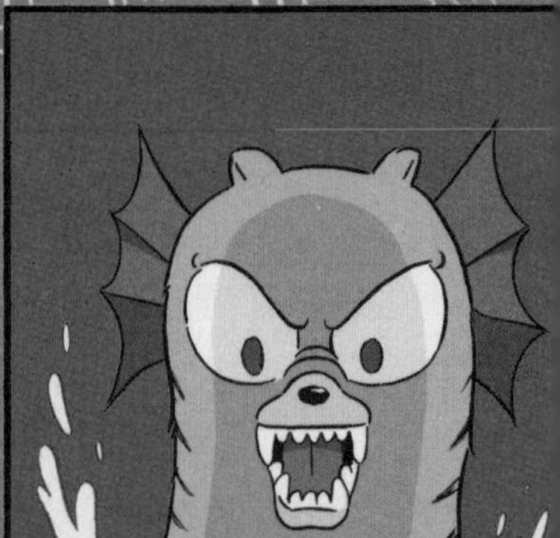

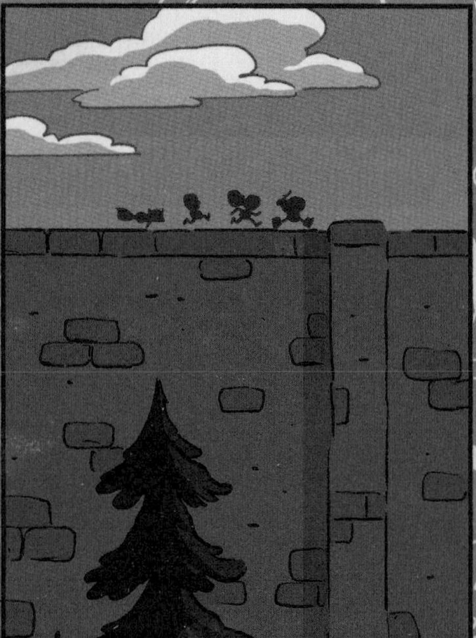

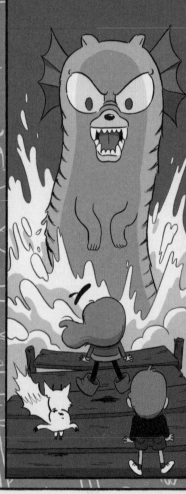

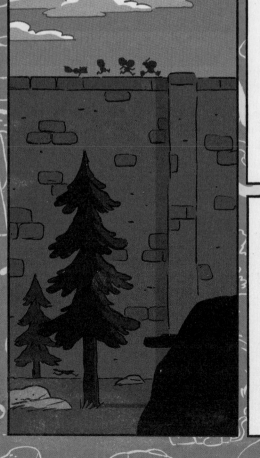

IN A MOMENT OF TENSION, BOTH HILDA AND HER MUM FIND THEMSELVES FLUNG FAR AWAY INTO A MYSTERIOUS, DARK FOREST – THE LAND OF THE TROLLS! CAN THEY WORK TOGETHER TO ESCAPE THE CLUTCHES OF THESE SINISTER STONE CREATURES?

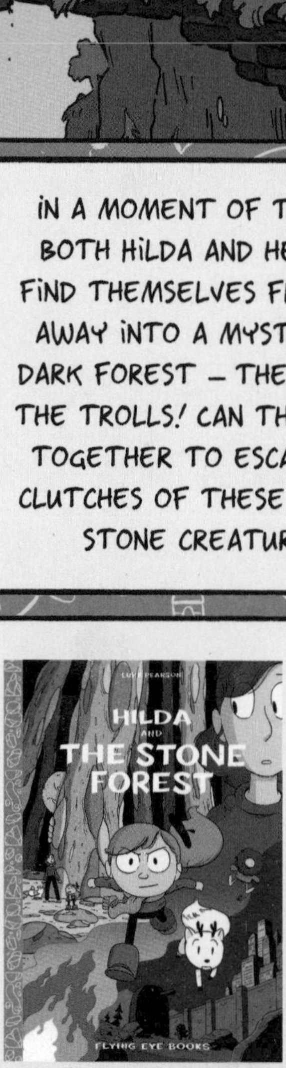
HILDA AND THE STONE FOREST
FLYING EYE BOOKS

HILDA AND THE STONE FOREST

ISBN 978-1-909263-74-1